Thous... ment ... flames. Bioroids were dropping, clearing a path for the Masters' flagship which was descending toward Macross's triad of mounds. Two towns at the outermost perimeter of the city had already vanished in a thermonuclear inferno.

Segmented appendages extruded themselves from the ship's underside. From each came a zigzag beam of light which cleaved the tallest of the mounds, displacing avalanches of debris, exposing the headless corpse of the SDF-1. The beams intensified and merged. But just when it was beginning to look as if the Masters were intent on resurrecting the fortress, the flagship powered down, tipped to one side, and exploded.

Then something even *more* unexpected occurred: a shaft of refulgent energy shot upward from the the SDF-1, somehow dampening the blast of the exploding starship. The SDF-1 itself was atomized and disappeared in what seemed to be a storm of swirling dust particles. In close-up they looked like seeds or *spores* being sucked upward and sent wafting in every direction as if being *sown* by the explosion.

Had the Earth been saved? Or had something more sinister been visited on the world?

By Jack McKinney
Published by Ballantine Books:

THE ROBOTECH™ SERIES:
GENESIS #1
BATTLE CRY #2
HOMECOMING #3
BATTLEHYMN #4
FORCE OF ARMS #5
DOOMSDAY #6
SOUTHERN CROSS #7
METAL FIRE #8
THE FINAL NIGHTMARE #9
INVID INVASION #10
METAMORPHOSIS #11
SYMPHONY OF LIGHT #12

THE SENTINELS™ SERIES:
THE DEVIL'S HAND #1
DARK POWERS #2
DEATH DANCE #3
WORLD KILLERS #4
RUBICON #5

ROBOTECH: THE END OF THE CIRCLE #18
ROBOTECH: THE ZENTRAEDI REBELLION #19
ROBOTECH: THE MASTERS' GAMBIT #20

Also by Jack McKinney:

KADUNA MEMORIES

THE BLACK HOLE TRAVEL AGENCY:
    Book One: Event Horizon
    Book Two: Artifact of the System
    Book Three: Free Radicals
    Book Four: Hostile Takeover

Books published by The Ballantine Publishing Group
are available at quantity discounts on bulk purchases
for premium, educational, fund-raising, and special
sales use. For details, please call 1-800-733-3000.

BEFORE THE INVID STORM

Jack McKinney

A Del Rey® Book

BALLANTINE BOOKS • NEW YORK

Sale of this book without a front cover may be unauthorized. If this book is coverless, it may have been reported to the publisher as "unsold or destroyed" and neither the author nor the publisher may have received payment for it.

A Del Rey® Book
Published by Ballantine Books

Copyright © 1996 by Harmony Gold U.S.A., Inc., and Tatsunoko Production Co., Ltd.

All rights reserved under International and Pan-American Copyright Conventions. Published in the United States by Ballantine Books, a division of Random House, Inc., New York, and simultaneously in Canada by Random House of Canada Limited, Toronto.

http://www.randomhouse.com

ROBOTECH is a trademark owned and licensed by Harmony Gold U.S.A., Inc.

Library of Congress Catalog Card Number: 95-92520

ISBN 0-345-38776-7

Printed in Canada

First Edition: April 1996

10 9 8 7 6 5 4 3

To supporters and critics met on the Internet: Todd Hill, Captain Harlock, PeterWW, Ethan P2144, Mondo Mage, Mad Mike, Miriya, Skull Leader, Ceej, and Breetai13, among numerous others.

AUTHOR'S NOTE

The definition of Protoculture that appears as the epigraph to Chapter Three paraphrases an anonymous posting that appeared on both alt.tv.robotech and AOL.sf.television.robotech. The choices of an Ikazuchi Command Carrier for Carpenter and a modified Garfish for Wolff were by consensus. The story itself grew from suggestions by Michael Riccardelli and Bill Spangler.

For historians, this book is meant to follow #9 of the original Robotech adaptations, and, as I see it, bridges the last gap in the series. That is not to say, however, that there aren't stories to tell about Zor, the Zentraedi, the Global Civil War, Macross Island, and the aftermath.

My work, in any case, is completed. So, a final thanks to "HAL"; Carl Macek; Tatsunoko Production Co., Ltd.; Harmony Gold; Comico, Eternity, and Academy Comics; Palladium and Donning Books; Del Rey Books; Risa Kessler; Ellen Key Harris; Steve Saffel; and everyone who read, wrote, reviewed, and retaliated.

CHAPTER ONE

As a species enslaved to time, we are wont to package history in tidy bundles. And so we find ourselves at the mercy of commentators who speak of First, Second, and Third Robotech Wars. And we are forced to listen to those same voices obsess about the generation of Henry Gloval, the generation of Rick Hunter, and the generation of Dana Sterling ... When, in my humble opinion, there was only the War that began with the arrival of the Zentraedi and ended with the departure of the Invid; and only one generation that lived through it: the generation of the lost.

Jacob Remy, *Robotech*

MISA YOSHIDA SIPPED GREEN TEA WHILE THE Robotech Masters' flagship fell to Earth, the whole of its starboard side aglow. A swarm of Logans and aged Veritechs trailed in seemingly slow-motion pursuit, like wrathful wasps spilled from some unseen orbital nest. Missiles of every conceivable type tore from the pylons and launchers of the reconfigurable fighters, fires blossoming against the instrument-studded backbone of the holed and deteriorating battlewagon. Silent explosions, both surface and internal, hurled building-size chunks of slagged alloy into Earth's already debris-littered atmospheric envelope. Some of the pieces struck and obliterated entire squadrons of Southern Cross mecha, but the chase continued unabated.

Veteran pilots of the First Robotech War could recall the devastation wreaked by the SDF-1 during its gradual dive to the surface, thirty-three years earlier. And the flagship—ravaged by fire and beckoned by gravity—was twice the size of that uninvited end-of-the-century visitor.

The digital feed from the robot news cameras was superb. Misa could almost believe that she was witnessing the scene through a viewport on one of the orbital weapons platforms, rather than watching it on wall-screen in the comfort of her spacious apartment in underground Tokyo. At twenty-two, she had only been alive for the catastrophic conclusion of the war against the Zentraedi, but she had often screened archival video of their attack on Macross Island, various encounters between the SDF-1 and the ships of Breetai's fleet, and, of course, the battle against the alien armada. Granted, scant footage had survived the Rain of Death, but nothing she had seen rivaled what the War Channel had been presenting since the arrival of the Robotech Masters, a year earlier.

Sometimes Misa found herself concerned that she didn't know what to do about the emotional desensitizing wrought by her hours and hours of viewing. A year ago she had been crying herself to sleep every night, but lately it seemed as if the war was taking place on a different world. Change channels and you could still find movies, sitcoms, sumo-bot wrestling, and exercise infomercials. In large part, that was because much of the war had been fought in space, and there was little any Earthbound citizen could do but support the efforts of the Army of the Southern Cross and shed nightly tears for the dead. In fact, most of the world was eager to perpetuate the illusion that what was happening above would have no impact on life below.

From the start, it had been assumed that the city targeted by the Masters would reap the whirlwind. While sovereign nation-states like Brasília, Mexico, and Rome had not been ignored by the Masters' weaponry, Monument City—in the Northlands—had taken the brunt of their ire. Headquarters of the United Earth Government, the Army of the Southern Cross, and the Global Military Police, Monument was without doubt the most important city in the world and arguably the most prosperous, though by no means the most populous. It also had the distinction of being the closest city to the war memorial that was thrice-born Macross, whose three Human-made buttes marked the resting places of the SDF-1 and -2, and the cruiser that had carried the Zentraedi warlord, Khyron Kravshera, to his death. And—as with the Zentraedi themselves—the SDF-1 had once been the property of the Masters, dispatched from their grasp by a renegade scientist named Zor.

Still, no one could explain why Tokyo, of all places, had escaped attack. Perhaps it was simply that the largely underground city hadn't offered much of a target for the Masters' laser cannons and lesser batteries. Or perhaps the Masters were under the impression that by sparing Tokyo they were sparing the life of Dr. Lazlo Zand, with whom they had been in brief contact three years earlier, and were unaware that Earth's chief Protoculturist had been relocated to Monument.

Whichever the case, Tokyo's exclusion from the war had only heightened Misa's sense of guilt; and so she kept the wallscreen on-line day and night, in the spirit of remote participation—to remain, if nothing else, *informed* about the war.

And just now the war was being brought down to Earth.

"We take you to the outskirts of Monument City," a news reporter was saying, "for an update on the latest in a series of ruinous developments . . ."

Misa set her tea aside and leaned toward the wallscreen.

Thousands of people were fleeing Monument—and with good cause, since a sizable portion of the city was in flames. Bioroids, the saucerlike mainstay of the Masters' fleet, were dropping in waves on Monument and on nearby Fokker Aerospace Base, clearing a path for the flagship, which was descending toward Macross's triad of mounds. Two towns at the outermost perimeter of the city had already vanished in a thermonuclear inferno.

The War Channel's use of the phrase "live from Monument City" struck Misa as ill-advised.

"And this just in . . . We have now confirmed earlier reports that Major General Rolf Emerson had been taken prisoner by the Masters. It now appears that the chief of staff of the Ministry of Terrestrial Defense has died inside the Masters' flagship, of wounds sustained aboard the *Tristar*, during yesterday's counter-offensive . . ."

She hugged herself and swung away from the screen, tears welling in her eyes as she stared out the window at subterranean Tokyo. She knew Emerson—indirectly, as it happened—through Southern Cross fly-boy Terry Weston. Terry had been Misa's roommate and constant though much older lover, until his recent reenlistment in the Tactical Armored Space Corps and his upside transfer.

More than the War Channel, it was Terry who had kept Misa and her closest friends apprised of the ASC's small victories against the Masters. These were victories that owed much to the efforts of the 15th Alpha Tactical Armored Corps, an elite Hovertank unit, which had engaged the enemy in space and on the ground, and on at least two occasions had infiltrated the enemy flagship itself. In command of the 15th was none other than Dana Parino Sterling, who, as well as being famous as Rolf Emerson's ward and the only offspring ever to result from a Human and Zentraedi mating, had also been a previous—and much younger—lover of Terry's.

At times, even Terry hadn't been able to separate the misinformation from the disinformation, but he had relayed to Tokyo whatever scuttlebutt reached his ears. For example, that the Global Military Police had managed to insert an espionage operative among the clone population of the Masters' ships. And that the Masters—until recently—had been tiptoeing around Monument City because of some Protoculture-manufacturing device concealed inside the SDF-1. The latest rumor to come down the well was that the Masters had issued an ultimatum to Supreme Commander Leonard that humankind either abandon Earth, or find itself caught in a war between the Masters and *their* enemies, the Invid.

If anyone could have negotiated an accord with the aliens, it would have been Rolf Emerson, Dana Sterling's guardian. And now Emerson was dead.

Tears coursing down her cheeks, Misa gazed absently at the huge fiber-optic display screen on the wall of the neighboring residential tower. The telepresence known as EVE had once dominated that and other screens, but EVE was long gone, gone with Zand and his Protoculture research facility, from which Zand's conversations with the Masters had taken place. With nothing but advertisements running on the screens ever since, was it any wonder that Misa preferred to stay tuned to the War Channel?

Moth to a flame, she returned her attention to the news ...

Dead, too, by all accounts, were Anatole Leonard and Chairman Wyatt Moran. Word had it that Leonard, the Supreme Commander of the Army of the Southern Cross, had blundered definitively at the end, and, by rejecting Emerson's plea to consolidate all ground-based forces, had allowed the Masters' flagship to slip through Monument's defenses.

Cameras positioned near the Macross memorial relayed a dazzling close-up of the spade-fortress, as three segmented appendages extruded themselves from the ship's underside. From each appendage came a zigzagging beam of light as bright as a solar prominence, which cleaved the tallest of the mounds, displacing avalanches of trees, boulders, and dirt from its flat top, ultimately exposing the headless corpse of the SDF-1 itself. The beams intensified and merged, and more of the dirt and debris that had been heaped on the Super Dimensional Fortress fell away or was incinerated.

But just when it was beginning to look as if the Masters were intent on levitating—if not resurrecting—the fortress, the flagship abruptly powered down, tipped to one side, and exploded.

Then something even more unexpected occurred: the explosion appeared to arrest itself. Misa thought that she had inadvertently activated the wallscreen's replay-and-pause function, but not a moment later a nova flared at the center of the cleaved mound and a shaft of refulgent energy shot upward from the SDF-1, engaging and somehow dampening the blast of the exploding starship.

Dampening, but not entirely containing the burst.

There was no way to stabilize the satellite-relayed image now. The ground was shaking with the force of an earthquake, and enormous fragments of housings, armor, and structural members were pelting the two standing mounds and the surrounding plain that had once been Lake Gloval. Atomized, the SDF-1 disappeared in what at first seemed to be a storm of swirling dust particles, but in close-up looked more like seeds or *spores*. Spores, and more: petals, leaves, flowers, entire plants—sucked upward and sent wafting in every direction, as if being *sown* by the explosion itself.

Misa gaped at the wallscreen, not knowing what to make of the sight. She reached a trembling hand for her cup of green tea and raised it to her lips. Had the Earth been saved—rescued one final time by the very ship that had started it all? Or had something more sinister than defeat been visited on the world?

Dana Sterling marched bravely at the head of the crowd, the side arm she had filched from Angelo Dante tucked into her broad leather belt, Polly the XT pollinator gamboling at her feet. She felt ravaged in every part of herself, burned raw, inside and out. Rolf Emerson, Leonard, and Moran—*dead*. The afternoon made colder by strange winds, born of the destruction of the Masters' flagship and the SDF-1 mound. The sky shrouded by black smoke from the funeral pyre that had been Monument City . . .

Behind her marched the rest of the 15th ATAC—
Angelo, Bowie, Sean, and Louie—along with Cosmic
Unit commanders Marie Crystal and Dennis Brown;
Global Military Police lieutenant Nova Satori; Musica,
Mistress of the Cosmic Harp; and the two hundred or so
alien clones the 15th had rescued from the Masters'
flagship.

In the east hung a great roiling cloud of spores and
petals that had been funneled into the upper atmosphere
by the destroyed flagship. Dana had come to think of
the mushroom cloud as a transfer station for the seedlings of the Flower of Life, a place of penultimate ap-
pointment where they hung until the winds dispersed
them worldwide. The physical and spiritual foodstuff of
the Invid, the Flowers of Life were harbingers of
Earth's next cataclysm.

To many it would appear that Zor Prime had died for
nothing, having sacrificed his life to prevent the Masters from retrieving the Protoculture Matrix hidden by
his namesake aboard the SDF-1. But Dana had been
granted a glimpse of a deeper truth—or at least she
thought she had. Mirroring the chaotic dance of the
spores overhead, images swirled in her mind, though
she couldn't say which were the by-products of real
events and which were flashbacks of hallucination.

Her recollection of those final moments aboard the
flagship were nothing less than dreamlike. The plum-
meting ship . . . Zor Prime's assassination of the Master
named Shaizan . . . Zor Prime's final words to her.
"They brought punishment down on themselves through
their misuse of the Protoculture, and I am the instru-
ment of that punishment, ordained by the Shaping."

The Shaping. Over the years she'd heard the term

bandied about by the disciples of Dr. Emil Lang and
Lazlo Zand, both of whom had turned Robotechnology
into a kind of religion, with Protoculture as its demi-
urge. But to hear the word from Zor Prime's lips . . .
Was he crazy at the end, she wondered, or merely a vic-
tim of the Protoculture?

Only moments earlier, on the flagship, as a consequence of touching a canister of the Protoculture, Dana
had had her own fling with madness: a vision of sorts,
fashioned of images lifted from events of the past year,
commingled with others whose origins she couldn't explain.

She recalled a green field, lush with the Flowers of
Life, surrounded by hills and vales—though only her
Southern Cross body armor and the distant, wind-
blasted crags gave any hint that she was on Earth. Dark,
cloaked figures had shown her a youthful image of herself and had intimated that she belonged to a triumvirate of clones, like those the Masters had created on
Tirol.

She had rejected the suggestion, even if it wasn't far
off the mark. She was, after all, half Zentraedi, and that
race of giant warrior clones had also been created by
the Masters. And, yes, there were many times when she
had tried to deny her ancestry, in the interest of fitting
in. But in the hallucination, rejecting the alien side of
herself had landed her in a bleak landscape, among
skulls and bones and the ash piles of ten thousand cre-
mations. Only to be rescued from her exile by a black-
eyed sprite of a girl, who was wearing a short, flowing
garment of gold and white, cinched at the waist by a
broad belt. A garland of woven Flowers of Life in her

hair, the sprite had introduced herself as the *other* child of Max and Miriya.

Dana's sister.

"Oh, Mother and Father will be so glad to know that I've finally made contact with you," she had said.

And Dana could recall thinking, *Finally?*

Around them were low crystal domes, and arching overhead was a purple sky hung with unrecognizable constellations. Faint music filled the air, reminiscent of the ethereal strains that emanated from Musica's Cosmic Harp. The sprite pressed a bouquet of Flowers into Dana's hands and hurried away to join two shadowy figures that had appeared on the scene.

Time grows short, one, or perhaps both of them, had sent to Dana without speaking. *So much has happened since our last contact with Earth, so many astounding things. Your powers are awakened now, and they are growing. Use them cautiously. We of the Sentinels are only beginning to understand the true nature of Protoculture.*

Okay. She had known about the Sentinels since Major John Carpenter's bumbling return from Tirol, months earlier. But was she supposed to accept that the hallucination's two shadows were her parents, who had apparently thrown in with that ragtag band of alien freedom fighters? Sounded like more of that nonsense about the Shapings. Even so, the sprite had given voice to a warning that was still ringing in Dana's ears. "Beware the spores, Dana. Beware the spores and the Invid!"

Dana had still been in the throes of the Protoculture-induced vision when Zor Prime had kissed her, scooped her up in his arms, and sealed her inside an ejection capsule, like she was some Lisa Hayes Hunter surrogate. Astounded by his actions, she sat frozen while he had secured the latch of the little, superhard alloy sphere and tasked it for launch. "I will allow no harm to come to your people," he had assured her.

But Dana had wondered during her slow descent to Earth, had Zor Prime been referring to Humans or Zentraedi?

The capsule had landed on the crest of a low foothill, atop which sat the Macross Scenic Overlook. It had puzzled her that Zor Prime should send her there, of all places, but then it dawned on her that she was meant to bear witness to his self-sacrifice and to the death of the Robotech Masters. And she had: curling herself into a ball when the flagship exploded; then railing at Zor Prime and the falling sky when the Protoculture Matrix had released the Flowers of Life from bio-stasis and seeded the world with their spores.

But she did so only for a moment. Because Lazlo Zand and Napoleon Russo had suddenly appeared on the scene, completely out of their skulls. Zand, who had had a fixation on Dana since her infancy, was vampirelike, displaying some sort of high-tech Dracula device, babbling about Dana's matchless powers, how they went beyond Protoculture, and how *he* would have them.

"First the power of Protoculture fills me," Zand had raved, "then the power of Dana Sterling. The Masters promised me that I would be wed to the Flower and I will not be disappointed!"

Polly, Dana's Cheshire cat of a pet, had shown up shortly after Zand had activated the device, but could do nothing as he trained it on Dana. The Protoculturist's own form enlarged, vibrating and contorting, while

Dana stood paralyzed and rotund Russo cowered like the little creep he was.

Across the plain, the Masters' flagship was coming apart and the genetic messengers of the Flower were gushing into a hellish June afternoon. Dana felt the tap of Death's bony hand on her shoulder and was on the verge of turning into the Reaper's embrace, when Zand loosed a howl of such agony and fright that even the Reaper retreated.

Zand had perhaps underestimated the dosage the device was feeding him, or somehow underestimated Dana's contribution to the influx of power. But either way, the net result was his transformation into a short-lived burst of radiant energy. And regardless, Dana wanted to believe that the outsize Flower of Life that took root where he had stood was actually him—Zand, wed to the Flower . . .

Arriving in a hijacked alien assault craft, the members of the 15th had found her there, stripped of her armor, Polly under one arm. Dana doing her *own* babbling about Zor Prime, the spores, the Invid, and a starship that she would someday pilot to wherever her parents were. But everyone had been patient with her, figuring that the nonsense she was spewing was the result of combat trauma. It was Dana's cry for Mommy, the orphaned generation's cry for all that had been denied them.

Nova Satori had brought her around. "Invid or no Invid, we have to report to whomever is in interim command," the intelligence officer had said. Plans had to be made, defenses set in place. No matter that Nova was cradling a clone infant in her arms.

Dana had composed herself and had ordered that the

escape capsule and the bottle-shaped assault craft be emptied of all rations and emergency supplies; and then she had grabbed Angelo's side arm and assigned herself the point position.

Renewed hope had eased the burden of the first couple of miles, but as the sky darkened and Monument's fire glow suffused the horizon, Dana felt herself sliding into despair. The brooding silence of the march told her that her squadron mates and the Tirolean clones were experiencing the same sense of loss.

"The war is over," Bowie had announced when he had stepped from the assault craft. And at the time she had been prepared to believe him. But now she wanted to respond, *"This* war—only this war is over." And suddenly there seemed so much to do . . .

But it would get done, Dana decided. The way all things got done: one step at a time. So she gritted her teeth, straightened her shoulders, and concentrated on planting one foot in front of the other.

CHAPTER TWO

Considerable irony attends the notion that, had the Masters been granted access to the Macross mounds and retrieved the Protoculture Matrix, they would have taken Earth as their own, unaware that their homeworld [Tirol], ravaged by the Invid, had subsequently fallen into the hands of the Robotech Expeditionary Force. Ironic or not, the theory is moot, in that enough evidence exists to suggest that the Masters, during their communications with Tokyo (i.e., EVE and Zand), had in fact been apprised by their Elders of developments in Tirolspace. Planetless, they most certainly would have claimed Earth, sowed it with the Flowers of Life, and moved on to some other world, leaving Earth—and whatever remained of humankind—to the Invid. In short, Earth was destined to play host to the Regis and her swarm, one way or the other.

Dominique Duprey, *Prelude to the Second Robotech War*

IN CONTRAST TO THE FANFARE THAT HAD ATTENDED THE interment of Macross City in 2015, the funeral for Zentraedi-founded Monument proved to be little more than a nod good-bye. No rousing speeches, no flag waving, no overflights by squadrons of mecha.

Rick Hunter and Max Sterling had flown with the Skull that spring day in Macross; Emil Lang, Lisa Hayes, and Vince Grant had offered remembrances. But Miriya Parino hadn't even been invited to attend the ceremony. She and two-year-old Dana had remained in Monument City, watching the memorial on TV. Monument had been Dana's home ever since, though it was Rolf Emerson with whom she had lived and not Max and Miriya, both of whom had left Earth in 2020, aboard the SDF-3.

Today many of Monument's Qwikform towers were still standing, but the core of the city was slagged, and it was without power and running water. Could the place be rebuilt, as Macross so often had? Probably. Though, what with the deaths of Leonard and Moran and the destruction of Fokker Base, ASC headquarters, the Senate Building, and the Presidential Palace, there seemed little point in doing so. Moreover, the slow exodus that had begun even before the Masters' arrival had resulted in a shortage of skilled workers.

The city would not be abandoned, however, because Denver, Portland, and many of the towns and villages that dotted the northwestern corner of the continent had closed their doors to immigrants. Many of Monument's residents would be forced to live in the ruins, guarding what little they possessed from roving bands of foragers, and praying that, if and when the Invid came, the aliens would select some other landscape to ravage.

As early as their march from the Macross mounds, Dana and the rest of the 15th had realized that there would be no saving the city, or, by the looks of things, the Army of the Southern Cross. Evidence of lawlessness and mass desertions could be found everywhere, in the form of looted stores and abandoned formfitting body armor and mecha. Too—though the war machines of the Masters lay silent in the streets, on rooftops, wherever they had crashed or gone to ground—the clones who had piloted the ships were found to have been executed by rogue civil defense units or butchered by mobs of vigilantes.

Greeted with such sights, Dana had ordered the rescued clones to discard their capes and tunics in exchange for ordinary Earthwear, and, at all costs, to keep their mouths shut. Plus, given that the barracks of the 15th ATAC hadn't survived the fires, she thought it best to avoid venturing too close to the city. Instead she led everyone to the mountainside log cabin she and Rolf Emerson had shared—along with Bowie Grant and Rolf's housekeeper, Sarah Willex—one structure which had survived the directed light of the Masters' weapons. There, they would make camp, at least until it could be determined who, if anyone, was in command of the city.

But when that determination was made, prospects for the future looked even darker than before. The mayor and the members of the City Council were dead. The half-dozen rear-echelon officers who had fled ASC headquarters short of the Masters' bull's-eye strike had, by default, been promoted to positions of authority. But the officer of highest rank to have weathered the war was ALUCE-based Major General Nobutu, and he and hundreds of TASC pilots had their hands full tending to the massive pieces of alien technology that remained in decaying orbits above the Earth.

On the political front, less than half the Senate had survived; and since many of those senators had been nothing more than the lackeys of various political factions, the so-called United Earth Government was effectively a headless entity.

Scarcely anything remained of the buildings in which Anatole Leonard and UEG Chairman Moran had died, let alone bodies. Even so, as information about Leonard's endtime equivocation began to emerge, the search for his remains took on a pathological frenzy. Many wanted to do to him what had already been done to countless Bioroid pilots. The power behind Chairman Moran's political throne, Supreme Commander Leonard was condemned even by the members of his general staff, who reviled the fact that he had gone down with his ship, as it were, and had not had the courage to answer for the miscalculations he had made.

Rumors abounded that Leonard had been in contact with the Masters two years prior to their actual attack. People argued that, regardless of who had fired the first salvo—Masters or Humans—the war could have been averted if Leonard had simply given the Masters access to the Macross mounds. But others felt that, while there was certainly some truth to the argument, it was just as likely that the Masters would have enslaved or exterminated Humankind once the Protoculture Matrix had been retrieved. In the end, history alone would pass judgment on the actions of the xenophobic Anatole Leonard.

Rolf Emerson, on the other hand, was being lauded as the war's true superstar. A champion of Zentraedi rights even during the Malcontent Uprisings of 2015–18, Emerson had showed himself to be an accomplished politician as well as a capable field commander. And more importantly, he had died a hero.

In the short time allotted to such things, Dana and Bowie had arranged a private observance for the man who had parented them through the long years of boarding schools and military academies to which they had been subjected. Rolf had cared so strongly about Earth's future that he had chosen *not* to ship with the Robotech Expeditionary Force on its diplomatic mission to Tirol, and had agreed to take Dana and Bowie as his wards, knowing full well that the SDF-3 might never be heard from again. These actions said more about his charitable nature than either of them could put into words, though they tried, nonetheless, speaking to the hundreds-strong crowd of senators, military officers, and plain folk who made the trek to the somewhat remote cabin.

Even Terry Weston, all but marooned at ALUCE, managed to send his condolences.

The first official meeting of the provisional Earth government took place two weeks after the destruction of the Masters' flagship, in Nueva Mesa, some two hundred miles south of Monument City. In attendance were those few senators who believed that something could be salvaged from the UEG—Barth Constanza, Alfred Nader, and Owen Harding, among others—and those few officers who nursed similar misconceptions about both the Army of the Southern Cross and the Global Military Police. Where such meetings had once convened in a vaulted hall of marble columns and adamantine floors, this one was held in a nondescript cinder-block building, which, in past incarnations, had housed a supermart and a cineplex.

After requesting a moment of silence for the dead the always outspoken Constanza brought the meeting to order. "I think our first order of business should be to determine whether we indeed have any business to discuss." The sturdily built Constanza spread his hands and regarded his confederates from his seat along the northern arc of the massive round table. "Ladies and gentlemen, I pose the question: Are we viable or not?"

"As a political body or a planetary species?" someone grumbled.

"Let's take them one at a time," Constanza said, maintaining his aplomb. "Is there a hope in hell that the nation-states of the world will voluntarily assign representatives to a global agency, or has it come down to every nation-state for itself?"

"The latter," Alfred Nader answered. He was a slight man with ruddy cheeks and a shock of white hair. "Speaking as a Southlander—though not for the Southlands—I can assure you that the policies of any global agency will be ignored. Oh, perhaps if such an agency were to situate itself in the Southlands, it might enjoy some limited respect. But even that much is in doubt. With the fall of Brasília, the last hope for a nucleus has been dashed. I'm afraid, Senator Constanza, that medieval attitudes hold sway from Mexico to Tierra del Fuego."

Everyone glanced at the fiber-optic world map that dominated the east wall of the vast, grimy space. Outside of the preemptive attack on Brasília and the intermittent harassing of Cavern City and Buenos Aires, the Masters had ignored the Southlands, where hundreds of agrarian-based polities had flourished since the defeat of the Zentraedi malcontents. Many of those polities had sworn allegiance to HEARTH, the Heal Earth Hajj, but as many others considered themselves nations in their own right, and rejected all attempts at enlistment in a global community.

"We could, of course, *compel* them to support a united government," Constanza suggested. "After all, we have the mecha."

The newly promoted General Vincinz, a former ASC staff officer, shot Constanza a withering look. "The

Southern Cross answered to Supreme Commander Leonard," he thought to point out, "not to the Senate."

Constanza returned the glower. "If you're implying that the presently leaderless Army of the Southern Cross is now autonomous, General, I suggest that you first poll the mechamorphs under your command. Those who haven't already deserted, that is."

Vincinz didn't proffer an immediate rebuttal. Some estimates put the desertion rate as high as 70 percent, and in at least half of those cases, the deserters had taken their mecha with them.

Across the table from Vincinz, General Nigel Aldershot, a seasoned veteran of the Robotech Defense Force, seemed to have anticipated the attention that was suddenly focused on him. "Let me assure all of you that the GMP will continue to act in the interests of global unity and will be quick to thwart the actions of any group that threatens that unity."

Made up of former Robotech Defense Force units and—much to the irritation of Supreme Commander Leonard—answering principally to the UEG, the Global Military Police had been formed after the attempted coup of 2029.

Aldershot glanced at the portly Vincinz. "Accept the fact that the *Army* of the Southern Cross has been dealt a serious blow, General. It might behoove you to abandon the separatist policies Leonard brought to the military."

"We're warriors first," Vincinz said, "politicians, never."

Constanza used his gavel to silence the arguments that broke out. "It's apparent that we've learned nothing from the divisiveness that split the Earth Defense Force after the launch of the SDF-3. Call yourselves what you will, Southern Cross or GMP. But bear in mind that you are the planet's only defenders. It rests in your hands, gentlemen, whether we engage the Invid—if they come—or roll over and show them our belly."

"They *will* come," GMP Major Alan Fredericks interjected. Second in command to Aldershot, Fredericks was lanky and pale, with prominent ears and long, flaxen hair. "That isn't tree pollen on the windowsills and on the cars. What you're seeing and sneezing at are spores of the Flower of Life—the Invid Flower of Life. Their Sensor Nebula has probably already registered the change in our atmosphere and relayed its findings to the swarm, wherever in the galaxy it is."

Originally dismissed as a spindrift cloud of interstellar dust that had somehow wandered into the Solar system from some impossibly distant region, the Sensor Nebula had made its appearance at the end of the war. Some of the assault ships of Rolf Emerson's strike force had actually passed through the leading edge of the cloud on their way to engaging the Masters' fleet. But it wasn't until the recordings of Leonard's conversations with the Masters had been decoded that the aberration had been correctly identified as an Invid Flower of Life sensor.

"Can't we simply destroy the thing?" Senator Stephen Grass asked. A muscular six-footer with a cunning smile, he had been a staunch supporter of the Army of the Southern Cross since its inception in Brasília during the Malcontent years.

Both Aldershot and Vincinz shook their heads. "The blasted thing has retreated to Mars orbit, where we can't get at it," Aldershot said. "It's as if it anticipated a threat."

"It exhibits signs of sentience," Fredericks elaborated. "And assuming that it can be destroyed, we'd need more than Logans or Veritechs to do the job. Something equal in firepower to a *Tristar*-class command ship. But even the least damaged of our frigates and fleet destroyers are going to require months of repairs."

"What about the enemy war machines?" Owen Harding suggested.

Again, Aldershot spoke for both the GMP and the Southern Cross. "First of all, most of them are depleted of Protoculture. Second, there's no figuring the damn things out. They seem to have been guided, in part, from the Masters' mother ships." He forced a weary exhale. "They're the junk in our new postwar landscape. Scaled-down versions of the husks of the Zentraedi cruisers we've been living with for twenty years."

Constanza cut him off. "Since these Flowers of Life seem to have taken such a liking to Earth, can't we matrix them, or whatever it is you have to do to them to extract Protoculture?"

Fredericks showed him a tolerant look. "I'm afraid that it's more complicated than that, Senator. In fact, with Dr. Zand dead, I'd hazard to say that there isn't anyone on Earth who would even know where to begin."

Vincinz drew attention to himself with a cough. "Speaking of Protoculture, I strongly suggest that we act quickly to consolidate all existing reserves—by force, if necessary."

"I concur with the general," Aldershot said.

Nader glanced at the two men. "I've heard rumors to the effect that many of the deserters left with their mecha."

Constanza nodded. "I've heard as much myself." He cut his eyes to Aldershot. "Suppose we enact a policy of amnesty. Every pilot who returns his or her craft will, in return, receive an honorable discharge. I mean, I understand these people not wanting to fight another day. Sometimes . . ."

The senator let the word dangle, and into the vacuum created by his silence poured the unstated anguish of every person seated at the table. Aldershot broke that silence after a long moment.

"Amnesty is a noble idea, Senator, but in order for it to fly, we need to have a government mandated to grant amnesty—which we don't—or an intact military to be discharged from—which we don't. Hell, we'd be better off offering bribes of food or scrip."

"We'll have no immediate need for the missing mecha if the Invid can be reasoned with," Nader said. "After all, we have no argument with them. And now both our races have fought the Zentraedi and the Masters."

Vincinz snorted a laugh. "Yes, and only *we've* beaten them."

Fredericks looked at him. "We didn't defeat the Masters. Zor Prime did." A quick glance around the table revealed that few were familiar with the name. "An enemy pilot the GMP managed to recruit and turn," he explained. "The alien took a . . . liking to Lieutenant Dana Sterling, and it was through him that Sterling and the 15th ATAC succeeded in infiltrating the Masters' flagship."

"Oh, so it was actually the GMP that won the war for us," Vincinz muttered with transparent sarcasm.

Fredericks narrowed his eyes. "I didn't make that claim. I'm only saying that Zor Prime brought the flagship down. And I have that on the authority of lieutenants Satori and Sterling, who were on board the flagship prior to its arrival at the mounds."

Constanza made a gesture of dismissal. "What's done is done. I'm interested in the Invid. Did this Zor Prime provide the GMP with any data about them?"

Aldershot grunted. "None that added appreciably to what we already know. Which is to say that they're mindless, sluglike things, nourished and driven by the Flower of Life, and that they've been at war with the Masters for generations. Does it sound to you like they can be 'reasoned with,' Senator?"

Nader made his lips a thin line and shook his head. "But I'm still of the opinion that it's important to have a governmental agency in place to negotiate with them, should the opportunity present itself."

Nader's statement met with murmurs of agreement.

"But where?" Constanza asked. He gestured broadly to the room's painted cinder-block walls. "To quote an old line, 'We can't go on meeting like this.' "

"It's senseless to reheadquarter ourselves in Monument," Harding said. "Not only for the obvious reason, but because the Invid may follow the Masters' lead in homing in on what's left of the Macross mounds. I recommend that we look to Detroit, Portland, or Denver."

Once more, the wall map became the focus of attention. All three of Harding's proposed sites had been hard hit by the Masters' Bioroids. A former mayor, Harding had pull in Detroit, though probably not enough to overcome the city's reluctance to house a re-born United Earth Government. Portland and Denver were long shots. The Southlands region was problem-atic because of the strong presence of HEARTH. But to what other cities could they look, where both satellite and microwave communications and military support were readily available? Africa and much of the Middle East remained nuclear wastelands; Europe was ravaged by disease; Asia and the Indian subcontinent were with-out technology; and Indonesia, the South Pacific, and Australia—with the exception of Sydney—had been parceled into dozens of separate sheikhdoms. Eventu-ally, everyone's gaze drifted to relatively unscathed Ja-pan.

As if reading the minds of his colleagues, Grass said, "There's always Tokyo. Even though it would mean dealing with President Misui ..."

Constanza was rubbing his chin when Grass looked at him. "It's not Misui that concerns me," Constanza said at last. "It's the people that run him."

"The Shimada Family," someone said.

Constanza nodded. "They kept their heads buried in the sand throughout the war, waiting for the day when we would come to them for help." He gave a brief look around. "I can't speak for the rest of you, but I for one am not ready to place the future of Earth in the hands of a family of *gangsters*."

CHAPTER THREE

Protoculture is the energy derived from the heat given off by the seeds of the Invid Flower of Life, when prevented by pressure from reproducing. The energy is produced by a process of cold fusion, when a lithium- and deuterium-rich solution permeates the seeds and their environs. A protein chain within the seeds themselves squeezes the lithium-6 and deuterium atoms into close proximity. Bosons, the resultant compressed atoms, are not affected by the effective repulsion of the Pauli principle. Only electrostatic barriers to fusion need be overcome. This solution, which also includes several seed-benificent nutrients, is known as the Protoculture Matrix . . . Maintained in bio-stasis, the seeds gradually surrender their stores of energy; the richer the lithium-deuterium solution, the quicker the depletion. For sustained energy, a moderate solution and moderate pressure are needed. However, as the solution begins to accrue carbon as a result of the fusion, the seeds receive nutrition sufficient to germinate. Thus, the Flowers end up consuming the matrix. And without the Invid or the pollinators to help fertilize the new growths that sprout in the containment vessels, the plants are effectively useless for the generation of energy.

Peter Walker, *The Truth Behind Protoculture*

ALL OF TOKYO WAS CELEBRATING THE END OF THE war, but nowhere were people rejoicing with as much zeal and abandon as on the rooftop of the Shimada Building. Once the sprawling though squat structure had accommodated Emil Lang's Robotech Research Center, and, years later, Lazlo Zand's Special Protoculture Observations and Operations Kommandatura. The building now encompassed the whole of the Koishikawa Gardens and towered over everything in aboveground Tokyo. Had the Masters launched an attack on the city, the Shimada would certainly have been ground zero; but Kan Shimada had gambled and won, and so the physical embodiment of his power and wealth had become symbolic of his complete mastery over Tokyo's surface and subterranean worlds.

The top of the building was a fanciful, five-story arrangement of unevenly yet artistically placed open-sided levels, linked by glass-booth elevators and Escheresque stairways, and lighted by massive skylights and fiber-optic arrays. Each hosted bird-filled gardens and shimmering waterfalls and ponds stocked with live carp. The war's-end fête was taking place on every level, though the uppermost was reserved for the elite among Kan-san Shimada's hundreds of invited guests.

Loosed from the streets below, tens of thousands of helium balloons were rising into Tokyo's warm night air, while brilliant fireworks blossomed over the Dream Archipelago landfill dumps that rose from the bay. Joyous people lined the roof's parapets, raising crystal goblets of vintage champagne, fresh from bubbling fountains. Others saluted the display—or the night, or perhaps the heavens—with bits of food plucked from tables replete with *mushi zushi*, sticky-rice cakes, *udon*, seaweed, shiitakes, lotus roots, omelets, fern shoots, and other "down-home" dishes.

Standing at the east parapet, Misa Yosida sipped champagne and ooh-ed and aah-ed with the rest of the well-dressed crowd as orange and blue umbrellas erupted in the southeastern sky. And she tried not to think too hard about the fiery demise of Monument City, footage of which was being run to death on the news channels. How she had come to be among the party's VIPs—rubbing elbows with the likes of President Misui and the members of the Diet—was a story that played like a fractured fairy tale, even when she recited it to herself on nights when the very reality of her circumstances made sleep impossible.

Misa was still the tall and voluptuous young woman she had been in her B.S. years—Before Shimada. But little else about her life was recognizable: not the balconied apartment underground, or the wardrobe and jewelry, or the number-crunching job with the Shimada organization. And the odd thing was that the transformation of her world owed less to the Robotech Masters than to a series of mishaps three years earlier that had landed her in the wrong place at the right time.

Landed not only her, but her closest friends, Gibley, Shi Ling, and Strucker. All three were present tonight on the top floor, and any one of them was more important to Kan Shimada's grand scheme than Misa was.

Now, if only Terry were here, the night would be complete, she told herself, looking up, not at the fireworks, but at the moon, where ALUCE Base was located. In the end, just before his reenlistment, physical contact between Terry and her had come down to point fighting in Onuma-sensei's dojo in Old Tokyo. But she went on loving him, and suspected that she always would.

"Some show, huh, gorgeous?" Strucker said, sidling up to her out of the crowd and smelling of scotch and potato chips. Blond and blue-eyed, he looked as if he had been imported from a different party. "Almost makes me nostalgic for life aboveground."

Misa looked at him askance. "The fresh air would probably kill you."

"You're right," Strucker hollered over the sound of distant reports. "Besides, I hear they have day and night up there."

Misa nodded. "It's true. The sun rises out of a cave in the east, and everything gets bright."

Strucker shuddered in elaborate disapproval.

When Misa had first met him, years back, he had been just another pimple-faced *otaku*—computer wizard—from the communal homes, who then went by the name Discount. But only the previous year he had learned the actual family name of his birth parents and so had dropped the self-styled sobriquet. An unexpected growth spurt that same year had brought him even in height with Shi Ling, but he was still only eye-to-mouth with Misa, and a good eight inches shorter than gangly Gibley. The sim-leather pants and vest made him appear less important than he was, but Misa, in a baggy velour suit, was no one to be throwing stones.

Shi Ling and Gibley wandered over while she and Strucker were talking, the pockets of their white utility coveralls bulging with pilfered foodstuffs and glass bottles of beer.

"Ah, to be rid at last of those *pesky* Masters," Gibley said, affecting a nasal, Northlands accent. "I was beginning to think they'd never leave."

"Leave?" Shi Ling said, playing along. "Why, I do believe they were *destroyed.*"

Gibley's big-knuckled fingers wriggled dismissively. "Please, dahling, don't bore me with details."

Hooked on end-of-the-century films, they made each other laugh, if seldom anyone else. The handsome and wiry Shi Ling, who had once called himself Census, was Chinese, but his parents had been in Japan during the Rain of Death, and he'd wound up orphaned in Tokyo. Gibley, though, was a Northlander, like Strucker, and pushing thirty-four.

An *otaku* of the first order, it was Gibley more than anyone who was responsible for the upgrade they'd all experienced, the outcome of an illegal run against Zand's Protoculture research facility, for whom Gibley had once worked. So there was some irony to his working in the facility once more—the expanded facility, to be sure—where he spent most of his time talking to machines. Not the way pilots did to their mecha via virtual-environment helmets, but actually *talking to machines.*

Misa was back to gazing at the moon when a pair of strong arms encircled her waist from behind and the owner of those arms pressed his right cheek to her left ear. "And I'll wager that Terry is looking straight at you right now."

She turned into Miho Nagata's embrace and kissed him on both cheeks, then stepped back to regard the dashing cut of his tuxedo and the luster of his leather wing tips. Even at forty-three, he looked better than the fireworks.

Misa's direct boss in the Shimada organization—her *kumi-cho*—Miho answered directly to *oyabun*, Kan Shimada. He had been promoted to gang boss in reward for the part he had played in Zand's downfall. Two years before the Masters had arrived in Earthspace, Gibley had sussed out that Zand was in communication—perhaps in league—with them, and Miho had successfully secured that information for the Shimada Family. In the wake of Zand's recall to Monument City, the Family purchased the phased Protoculture facility—

lock, stock, and barrel—and had installed Gibley to head up research into what Gibley termed "machine mind." At the same time, Kan Shimada had parlayed knowledge of the Masters' imminent arrival into a vast enterprise, by discouraging the development of surface Tokyo—including the construction of a Southern Cross base—and encouraging the immigration to underground Tokyo of select individuals from all over the world.

Misa suspected that she had been taken under the Shimada wing primarily because she reminded Kan of Yoko Nitabi, his adopted daughter who had been an operative within Zand's operation, and whom Zand had had executed. Her talent for numbers notwithstanding, only Misa's resemblance to the late Yoko could explain why she, too, had people answering to her—even if they were only money-drinkers and errand boys. Thus she occupied a top position in the traditional *yakuza* ranking, with a curious twist, in that working at or near the top now meant living at the bottom—in the underground—while working at or near the bottom meant living at the top, in the realm of *okage*—expendable—surface Tokyo.

Similarly, the end-of-the-century portrayal of the *yakuza* as full-body-tattooed mobsters was as period an image as that of the sword-wielding samurai. While the organizational hierarchy had been maintained, the goals of the organization had been legitimized. Where once only the dumbest of street boys were employed to run errands, the Shimada Family now employed only the brightest—and not to busy themselves with motorcycle thefts, drug dealing, or pimping, but assist in the even more profitable business of *political* control. Softened, as well, was the policy of racial purity that had characterized the crime families of the twentieth century. The survival of Tokyo was given central prominence, for the city had come to represent the ark that would carry Humankind into the future.

Miho was exchanging back-clapping embraces with the guys and making fun of Gibley's and Shi Ling's outfits, though that didn't dissuade him from accepting the bottle of beer Gibley conjured from the front pocket of his coveralls.

"Kanpai!" Miho said, lifting the bottle before chugging half of it. "Now if we can just get through the next war." He chugged what remained of the bottle and patted his full lips with a monogrammed handkerchief.

His comment strained the levity of the moment, but only briefly. "How many years do you figure we have before the Invid come calling?" Gibley asked. "We went twenty between the Zentraedi and the Masters."

"I'm guessing ten," Strucker said.

Shi Ling shook his head. "No way. Five, tops."

Gibley held up three fingers, and glanced at Miho.

"Mr. Shimada has reason to believe that the Invid will be here within the year."

Misa's jaw dropped. "Do you think he's right?"

Miho draped a comforting arm around her shoulders. "We're in the process of investigating some data that has come to us from associates in what's left of Monument City. It seems that the Invid have moved some sort of Protoculture sensor into our planetary neighborhood. That suggests that they are on the way. But I say, the sooner they arrive, the sooner we get to clear the air—so to speak."

Gibley shook his head uncertainly. "I don't know that Tokyo will be as lucky next go-round."

"Our survival had nothing to do with luck," Miho said.

"Sure, by keeping the Southern Cross away, we managed to keep the Masters away," Shi Ling said. "But the Invid may not be as discriminating about which cities they target."

"True," Miho allowed. "But our prominently displayed offering may give them pause."

"Offering?" Misa said.

Miho trained his smile on her. "Flowers of Life. To be gathered from places throughout Asia and the Pacific Rim nations and brought here, to Tokyo. We might even gift wrap them."

It surprised no one on Nova Satori's recovery team that Lazlo Zand's research laboratory was filled with the Flowers of Life; after all, Zand was believed to have been ingesting them since the late teens, when isolated clusters had begun appearing in the Southlands. Rumors persisted that he had even managed to fabricate a miniature Protoculture Matrix. But, no, what Nova's team found surprising—*remarkable*—was that the laboratory was at all intact. Cached among the amorphous buildings of the military-industrial complex that adjoined Fokker Aerospace Base, outside Monument City, the small L-shaped cell had sustained a near-direct hit that had flattened everything around it. But it figured that Zand would have had the place secretly hardened—in all probability to the detriment of its close neighbors.

It figured, too, that Zand would have had the lab wired for self-destruction, which was why Nova had sent a bomb squad in advance of her team. Several devices had been disarmed, and yet, despite the caution exercised in opening a hole in the wall—no one dared use the single, reinforced-alloy door—undetected devices had flooded the interior with a gas that was not only lethal to living things but corrosive to the lab's library of conventional and optical data-storage tapes and diskettes.

Once again, though, Nova had second-guessed Zand. Outfitted in antihazard suits, everyone on the team had been ordered to rush into the lab and grab whatever they could lay their gloved hands on, without wasting time on assessments.

Much of what was recovered was irreparably corrupted long before it reached the GMP's transitional headquarters, south of Denver. Then came the daunting task of analyzing and deciphering Zand's encryption techniques. The codes used to encrypt some of the data proved unbreakable, but GMP specialists chanced on the discovery that Zand had frequently employed the code he had used in his Tokyo-Monument communications with Anatole Leonard. Among the latter data was what seemed to be a partial biography of the Tirolean scientist, Zor. The biography had perhaps been gleaned from dialogues with the mother computer Emil Lang had removed from the SDF-1 before the Zentraedi had come looking for the ship, and which had provided the voice and image for Tokyo's youth-friendly telepresence, EVE. There were also hints of some compromised surveillance operation that had involved Zand, Leonard, and the Robotech Masters, along with several members of the Shimada Family.

Other tapes and disks contained transcriptions of Zand's initial meetings with Leonard, back in the teens, and subsequent meetings that were attended by Wyatt

Moran and T.R. Edwards, then in the employ of a covert UEG agency.

However, the real prize among all that encrypted treasure was the data on the Invid and their precocious Flowers, which Lang either hadn't had access to or hadn't shared with the UEG prior to the launch of the SDF-3. It was conceivable that Zand had retrieved the information from the mother computer, but just as conceivable that the information had arisen a priori through Zand's intimate acquaintance with the Flowers of Life.

Last but not least was the directory—if not the files—devoted to Zand's blatantly obsessive fixation on Dana Sterling. Dana's childhood predilections, Dana's adolescent comings and goings, Dana's misadventures in the Academy, Dana's performance on the battlefield . . .

Nova cursed her bad luck in not having recovered those files. But if nothing else, Nova still had access to Dana. And if Dana was even half as important to Earth's future as Zand had seemed to think, then the time had come to put Dana to the test.

CHAPTER FOUR

Mars Base had had its ups and downs over the decades. Founded just after the turn of the century, Sara Base—as it was then known—was already in ruins by 2010, when the RDF engaged the forces of Khyron's Botoru Battalion on the Martian surface. Rebuilt in 2016, during the readying of the SDF-3, the base was abandoned in 2022, only to be resurrected two years later, deriving most of its funding from a conglomerate of Asian concerns. It has been suggested that its closing, in 2030, was the direct result of the Shimada Family's advanced knowledge of the imminent arrival of the Masters; for, shortly thereafter, the upper management of each of those Asian concerns relocated to subterranean Tokyo.

From the introduction to Shi Ling's
Sometimes Even a Yakuza Needs a Place to Hide

THE EMERSON PROPERTY HAD BECOME AN ARMED camp. Western larch and pine from the higher elevations had provided lumber for six watchtowers, all of which were linked by a tall palisade crowned with concertina wire. Behind the stake fence stood three Hovertanks, which had been found abandoned in Monument City. Named *Livewire II*, *Bad News II*, and *Trojan Horse II* after the mecha the 15th had had to leave aboard the Masters' flagship, the squat, reconfigurable tanks, with their thruster pods and down-sloping prows, had belonged to the 13th ATAC and were running on empty. Louie, Sean, and Angelo were in charge of the mecha, while the towers were manned by the more militant triumvirates of the clones from Tirol. Though in command of the camp, Dana and Bowie had refused to so much as don armor, much less arm themselves.

It had been when Dana had proposed the cabin as an alternative to Monument City that the original band had splintered. Marie Crystal and Dennis Brown had been eager to learn what had become of the Black Lions, and Nova, of course, had felt compelled to report to GMP headquarters—whether it was standing or not. So when Nova later showed up at the cabin, seated at the controls of a GMP personnel carrier, the first thing Dana asked her was, "Are you out for a joyride, Lieutenant, or is that APC your new office?"

"Just release the gate and let us inside, Dana," Nova said from the opened driver's-side door. "We're here on official business."

Dana made no move to unbolt the reinforced gate. "Official? On whose authority?"

"On the authority of the provisional government."

Every Human within earshot on the secure side of the perimeter laughed.

Nova and Dana had a long history of such clashes, dating back to Nova's first visit to the cabin some three years earlier, as a mouthpiece for Nigel Aldershot and his coterie of RDF dissidents. She had come then to enlist Rolf's support for a planned coup against the Southern Cross. But something about Nova had roused Dana's competitive instincts then, and it had been that way between them ever since.

Throughout the war, they had had run-ins over procedures and protocols; but their rivalry hadn't peaked until Zor Prime entered the scene. After being debriefed by the GMP, the seemingly amnesiac alien defector had been attached to the 15th ATAC, where his actions could be monitored. And both Dana and Nova had fallen in love with him.

"Lieutenant Sterling, you are in violation of UEG decrees by harboring prisoners of war," Alan Fredericks announced as he climbed from the APC. "The clones you captured aboard the flagship have to be debriefed—either by the GMP or Southern Cross Intelligence. You decide."

Dana directed a calming gesture to the nervous Tiroleans in the nearest tower, then swung to face Fredericks. "War's over, Major—or hadn't you heard? These people are asking for political asylum. Which means that they'll only deal with a recognized member of the 'provisional government.'"

Nova stepped out of the vehicle and approached the gate. "General Vincinz isn't going to be as patient with you as we are, Dana."

"*General* Vincinz? Last I remember, he was a colonel—and not a very competent one. And we're not about to kowtow to some *default* commander." Dana grimaced. "As if Leonard wasn't bad enough."

"Be reasonable, Sterling," Fredericks said. "We agree with you about Vincinz—and Leonard—but these clones—"

"These 'clones' saved our asses, Fredericks." Dana glanced at Nova. "Tell him, Nova. You were there."

Fredericks rolled his eyes. "That's like saying that the SDF-1 saved us."

Dana's expression hardened. "Tell him about Zor Prime, Nova. His last words were that no harm would come to Earth. And he kept his promise. *He* destroyed the flagship." She lowered her voice. "He couldn't have known that his actions would wind up spreading the spores."

Nova was quiet for a moment; then she walked to the gate. "Remember how some people were crediting Breetai with helping to end the war against Dolza? It's the same thing, Dana: Maybe the Tiroleans did help, but it was too little, too late. And now we need to talk to them about the Invid. Surely, as a commanding officer, you can see the importance of that."

Dana folded her arms across her chest. Behind her, Bowie, Angelo, Sean, and Louie were advancing. "I've resigned my command."

"You've deserted, you mean," Fredericks snapped.

"No, I've resigned—from the killing." She looked at her squadron mates. "That goes for all of us."

Nova's heart-shaped face reddened. "Then you should surrender your Hovertanks. The UEG is appropriating all mecha and supplies of Protoculture. Any attempt to seize or withhold Protoculture will be treated as treason."

Angelo Dante planted his hands on his hips. "You can't seriously believe that people are going to honor that edict. With the Southern Cross being held accountable for the war? Oh, sure, if the SDF-3 suddenly appears out of spacefold, then maybe you'll see ex-soldiers surrendering their mecha. But until then, you don't have a prayer. Not here, and definitely not in the Southlands. While you're standing here arguing with us, people are stashing Protoculture wherever they can."

Nova considered it, then smiled ruefully. "Then why all this—the fence, the watchtowers, the Hovertanks—if you've resigned from killing?"

"Killing and defending are two different things,"

Sean Phillips answered. Tall, with the rugged good looks of a swashbuckler, he had once lived and breathed for Nova, but there was little evidence of that in the stare he showed her now.

Fredericks snorted disdainfully. "And what about the Invid?"

Dana thought about the hallucinatory vision she had had aboard the flagship. *Beware the spores*, the sprite had told her. *Beware the Invid* . . . but she wasn't about to start rambling as she had at the Macross mounds. "When the Invid come, a lot of people are going to fight and die for nothing," she said. "There's something inevitable about the outcome of the next war. I don't think we could win it, even if we had the SDF-3 at our backs."

Nova was shaking her head, her long mane of black hair flowing. "I can't believe what I'm hearing. You're giving up. You're ready to surrender the planet to the Invid."

As well as they thought they knew her, even the members of the 15th were stunned by Dana's response.

"Yeah. In a sense, I guess I am surrendering the planet. But only because my destiny requires that I take a different path." She cut her eyes to Louie. "*My* destiny. No one else's."

Fredericks gazed at her questioningly. "It almost sounds like you know some way out of this mess."

Dana started to speak, but bit back the words. "I, I can't explain."

"You're going to head for the hills, is that it?"

Dana compressed her lips and remained silent.

"Well, personally, I don't care where you end up," Nova said at last. "But before you go, there are two missions that only you can execute—and neither bears on the fate of the Tiroleans. So at least hear us out, Dana. You owe us that much."

Dana disagreed, but opted not to debate the point. "Start talking," she told Fredericks.

The GMP major stepped forward. "*General* Vincinz has dispatched lieutenants Marie Crystal and Dennis Brown to Space Station Liberty, with orders that the station should attempt to reestablish contact with the factory satellite."

The tankers of the 15th exchanged baffled looks. The moonlet-size facility had departed Earthspace three years earlier, under the stewardship of several hundred Micronized—downsized—Zentraedi. It had not been their aim to escape the Masters, but to serve as a decoy. The destruction of the factory was to have alerted Earth that the Masters had arrived in the Solar system. The Masters, however, had either overlooked the factory or chosen to ignore it.

"Liberty will advise the Zentraedi that the Masters have been defeated," Fredericks was saying, "and that we want them to return to Earth."

"But, why?" Dana asked in disbelief. "Not to defend us against the Invid—"

"Yes—in a way," Nova said. "We want their help in destroying the Sensor Nebula."

Fredericks glanced at Nova, then Dana. "The Flowers of Life are taking root faster than we can eradicate them. The damned things have a will of their own. It's as if the spores are deliberately seeking out the most arable areas of the world—the Northlands plains, Venezuela, northern Argentina, central Europe ... Research and Development is trying to develop a sensor so that we can go after them with Logans and such, but so far no one's had much success."

Nova exhaled with purpose. "The Flowers seem to be some type of tripartite, pollen-producing angiosperm, but they disperse spores, which should classify them as gametophytes. And yet, even what we're calling spores turn out to be more like seeds, which resemble minuscule parasols."

Dana quirked her brows together. "But how's the factory supposed to destroy the Sensor Nebula, when it isn't even armed?"

"By transporting one of our crippled destroyers in its belly," Fredericks explained.

Dana gave it some thought. "It won't work."

Nova and Fredericks spoke at the same time. "Major Carpenter seems to think it will work."

Dana gave her head a mournful shake. Barely emerged from spacefold, the REF commander had erred tactically by engaging the Masters' fleet and losing his ship. "You're going to trust what he says? The man's space happy."

"You trusted him enough to believe what he had to say about the Expeditionary mission and the Sentinels," Nova pointed out.

"That has nothing to do with it."

Fredericks was eyeing Dana with suspicion. "Do you have specific data relating to the Sensor Nebula that we haven't seen?"

Dana shook her head. "I shouldn't have said that the plan won't work. What I mean is, that it won't matter. The Invid will come."

"Not if their beacon is destroyed."

Fredericks' tone of voice told Dana that the matter

had already been decided. "All right, so you're recalling the factory satellite. How does that concern me?"

Nova and Fredericks traded brief glances. "We want you to serve as our emissary," Nova said. "We want you to persuade the Zentraedi to help us."

"You're practically one of them," Fredericks added. "So it stands to reason ..."

Dana laughed—not because there was anything funny about the proposal, but because Nova had asked the same of Rolf on the day she and Dana had met—even though Rolf wasn't *one of them*. General Nigel Aldershot had hoped that Rolf could entice the remaining Zentraedi to side with the Robotech Defense Force in a coup against the Southern Cross.

"Assuming for the moment that you can convince the Zentraedi to return, I'll accept the assignment," she told Nova, "in the spirit of old times. Now, what's this other business I'm uniquely suited for?"

"It involves Lieutenant Terry Weston," Fredericks said, taking delight in Dana's surprised reaction. "It's come to our attention that Weston enjoys considerable cachet among the *yakuza* organization that purchased Lazlo Zand's research facility in Tokyo. We have information that Shimada's researchers have found a way to interface with machines, without the need for Proto-culture."

"Your past relationship with Weston is no secret," Nova interjected. "We've recalled him from ALUCE to serve as your introduction to the Shimada Family and the researchers they employ." She turned to Louie Nichols, who immediately pushed his goggles up onto his forehead. "In the interest of opening a scientific dialogue with Tokyo, we want Corporal Nichols to accompany you."

Though battered and bruised by the Masters, Space Station Liberty still hung at its Trojan Lagrange point, close to the moon. For more than ten years Liberty had combined the functions of outpost fortress, communications nerve center, and way station along the routes to ALUCE and Mars Base—now closed. Its complex communication apparatus—apparatus that wouldn't function as well downside—was Earth's only method of maintaining even intermittent contact with the factory satellite.

Marie Crystal and Dennis Brown had been on board for close to a week now, awaiting orders from Southern Cross command to drop back down the well or to continue on to ALUCE, which was where they both wanted to be. But it was becoming obvious that Vincinz was no more capable of commanding the Army of the Southern Cross than Senator Barth Constanza was the "provisional" Earth government. Where Crystal and Brown initially had been given to believe that Liberty would constitute nothing more than a brief stopover, orders received since then made it appear that they were being permanently reassigned to the station, while at the same time they were being considered for the Sensor Nebula mission, should the Zentraedi agree to it.

Frustrated by the slew of contradictory transmissions from Southern Cross temporary headquarters in Denver, the two lieutenants had whiled away the week effecting repairs on their Logans, jogging on the track retrofitted into Liberty's "handle"—for the station resembled a colossal version of a child's rattle—and trying hard to maintain objectivity in an atmosphere steeped in paranoia.

Sitting duck that it was, Liberty was your posting only if you'd scored brilliantly on no less than twenty psychological tests *and* you had been evaluated by a dozen psychologists, neurometric analysts, and behaviorists. Still, the recent war had taken a toll on everyone aboard, and, what with the Invid lurking in Earth's imminent future, there wasn't a watch officer or communications tech who hadn't been placed on a regimen of mood elevators or mild tranquilizers. All it took now was a hunk of war debris turning up as paint on some radar screen and the station went to full alert. The turrets that concealed the gleaming snouts of Liberty's twin- and quad-barreled batteries were never closed, and the threat-assessment boards and signal-warfare countermeasures computers were serviced twice a day, lest some glitch allow the Invid to arrive in the Solar system undetected.

Despite her best efforts, however, Marie was growing frazzled. When she regarded herself in the mirror, her normally pale skin looked positively ashen; her oblique blue eyes—which people liked to call exotic—were bloodshot; and her black hair appeared more intractable than unruly. ALUCE notwithstanding, she would have preferred ridding local space of the Masters' depleted hover platforms and assault ships over pacing Liberty's narrow, duct-lined corridors waiting for orders that might never come.

Dennis didn't have to say as much in order for Marie to recognize that he felt the same. Until three weeks earlier, they'd only known each other as fellow unit commanders in the Black Lions. But then came the hastily planned mission to rescue Rolf Emerson from the crippled *Tristar*, and their subsequent capture by the Robotech Masters. Marie could recall every detail of those events: the *Tristar*'s ruined bridge; Emerson's blood, puddled on the command chair; the metallic smell of the cramped, alloy-armored ejection module; the maw of the Masters' flagship; the eerie tonality of their voices . . .

Will you make your species see reason and surrender? one of the monkish-looking Masters had asked them. *We cannot allow your stubbornness or the fate of one tiny world to endanger the establishment of our Robotech universe. Your small-mindedness merely illustrates how primitive you are . . .*

She couldn't help but wonder whether the Invid would soon be posing the same questions and uttering the same condemnations; and whether some new Rolf Emerson would arise to inform them that Humankind would never surrender their world, and that what didn't kill us only made us stronger.

The Masters had communicated with the 15th ATAC in the hopes of orchestrating a hostage exchange: their two prize defectors—Zor Prime and Musica—for the lives of Emerson, Marie, and Dennis. But no honest accord had been reached. No sooner had the Hovertanks of the 15th been brought aboard the flagship than all hell had broken loose, and Emerson had been killed. It was his death, perhaps more than any other single event, that had forged the bond between Marie and Dennis, and as well between Marie and Dana Sterling, with whom she had been at odds nearly from the day Dana had graduated from the Academy and had been appointed acting CO of the 15th ATAC.

Dana came to mind now, as Marie was staring over the bony shoulder of a communications tech named Rawley, who had called to screen several real-time views of Earth's North- and Southlands. Following the destruction of Macross City, Dana's father, Max Sterling, had helped rid the Southlands of malcontent Zentraedi. But several hundred acculturated Zentraedi had allied themselves with the REF and shipped for Tirol aboard the SDF-3. Still others had exiled themselves on the factory satellite. Marie asked herself how she might feel if she were Dana, knowing that her people, so ill-treated under the reign of Chairman Moran and Supreme Commander Anatole Leonard, had now been asked to lend support in the fight against the Invid.

"I've seen turn-of-the-century recon-sat opticals," Rawley was saying, "and I swear you'd think you were looking at a different world." A sharp-featured man of about twenty-five, he had long, narrow hands and an enormous Adam's apple, which bobbed when he spoke. "Just here," he continued, indicating the bulbous northeast coast of the Southlands, "all this used to be dense forest, fronted by sandy beaches. Now it's wasteland— as devastated as anything in Africa or Asia."

"The Rain of Death," Marie said, referring to the assault by the Zentraedi Grand Fleet in 2012, the catastrophic conclusion to the Robotech War.

"The *Zentraedi* Rain of Death," Rawley amended nastily. "And now we're inviting them back." He shook his head disapprovingly and called new views to screen.

While newborn Marie had lost her family to the Rain, she had never really known them, and so had no feelings one way or another about the Zentraedi—an attitude not uncommon among the so-called orphaned generation. "We need their help," she told Rawley.

"But how do we know they haven't gotten that factory on-line again, spitting out Battlepods or other armed craft? How do we know they're not going to blow us out of orbit just for suggesting that they side with us against the Invid?"

For the first time, Marie noticed that Rawley's hands were trembling slightly and that his upper lip was beaded with sweat. "From what I've heard, the Zentraedi aren't especially conversant with technology."

Rawley stared at her, wide-eyed. "From what *you've* heard? Well, maybe you should research what they accomplished during the Malcontent Uprisings, Lieutenant. You might feel differently about the transmissions you forced us to send."

In the first place, Marie told herself, no one had been *forced* to do anything. But you didn't point that out to a guy who needed to have his medication dosage increased. And as for the flash message Liberty had transmitted, in addition to the recall code, it had contained nothing more than a schedule of the Reflex burns the factory would be required to make in order for it to insert in Earth orbit. The trajectory corrections had been based on Dr. Emil Lang's original calculations.

"If the Zentraedi respond to our request," Marie said finally, "they'll do so as comrades, not—"

"Paint!" Rawley rasped, shooting to his feet and leaning over the console, practically nose to nose with the vertical threat-assessment board. "I've got major paint on long-range two!" he said into a pickup, spewing coordinates, even while his left hand was fumbling

with the release key for the alert-status activation display.

Marie studied the assessment board as sirens began to blare throughout the station. Rawley pressed his headset against his ear and adjusted the gain on one of the transceivers. "I'm waiting for identification!" he yelled into the microphone. "I have high probability that it's an alien ship! Invid, it has to be Invid!"

A massive, radish-shaped object took shape on the friend-or-foe display. "It's the satellite!" Marie said, caught up in the emotion of the moment.

And the next words to issue over the speakers were Zentraedi.

CHAPTER FIVE

"We'd heard rumors about Louie Nichols, nothing more than that. For instance, we knew he'd been credited with detecting the bio-magnetic field deployed by the Masters' fortresses, which led directly to the grounding of their flagship early on in the war. I mean, if it hadn't been for that, the Southern Cross might never have realized just who or what they were up against. Then, of course, there was Louie's 'pupil pistol'—his targeting glasses. We had no doubts that he'd fit in. In fact, we probably would have kidnapped him if he'd turned down Mr. Shimada's offer to join our team."

Wilfred Gibley, quoted in Bruce Mirrorshades'
Machine Mind and Arthurian Legend

"**G**ATH YAR, DENTALLA!" DANA YELLED AS she bounded across the arrival gate at Tokyo's Haneda ("Big Bird") Airport and hurled herself at Terry Weston. The Zentraedi phrase—one her mother had shouted at her repeatedly during her childhood—translated as "Complete the mission, ally," but Dana used it the way Miriya Parino had, meaning, "Pick up after yourself!"

Terry fended off a flurry of Dana's kicks and punches before she managed to sneak one past him. Months of piloting a Veritech against the Masters' hover platforms had sharpened his mind but slowed his Earthbound reflexes.

Neither he nor Dana were in uniform. Terry wore black jeans, fly-boy boots, and a tight-fitting shirt; Dana, leggings, a baggy top, and vest. Blond and lanky,

Terry was nearly twice her age, but could have passed for a slightly older sibling. Louie Nichols, in a tanker's mechasuit and his ever-present tinted goggles, was the only one who looked the part of a combat veteran.

Following the backhand that tagged him lightly on the chin, Terry pulled Dana into an affectionate embrace and held her until she had calmed down. The point/counterpoint was a habit with them, still operational after all these years. Eventually he stepped back to regard her, though guardedly. "How much of what I've been hearing about you and the 15th is on the level?"

Dana made her arching brows bob. "Tell me what you've been hearing."

"That you were aboard the flagship minutes before it exploded."

"Guilty as charged."

"And that it was you who turned the red Bioroid pilot against the Masters."

Dana's grin faltered. Terry was referring to Zor Prime. "Umm ... No, I can't take credit for that. The red Bioroid pilot did what he needed to do. I just happened to be there when he did it."

Terry shook his head in amazement. "Next, they'll be erecting a monument to you."

"Not likely," Dana said, ready to change the subject. She turned to Louie. "Terry, Louie Nichols."

Weston extended his hand. "Good to meet you, Nichols." When his gaze returned to Dana, the mirth had left his eyes. "I was sorry to hear about Rolf."

Dana compressed her lips and nodded. "Rolf's the one who deserves a monument."

"How's Bowie taking it?"

"Not good. But he found someone who's helping him

through it." She didn't bother to add that that someone was a green-haired alien clone named Musica.

The Shimada Family had provided a stretch limousine, which was waiting curbside. Dana had been told to expect as much, but the car took her by surprise nevertheless. The Terry Weston she knew was a rough-and-tumble guy who rode motorcycles and piloted Veritechs. And while he maintained that he still rode a vintage Marauder, he seemed awfully at home in the air-conditioned comfort of the backseat.

"Just why did you agree to play go-between for the Shimadas and the Southern Cross?" Dana asked him when they were under way and the privacy partition had been raised. "After what the Cosmic Units accomplished upside—in spite of Leonard—you sure don't owe command anything above and beyond the call."

"I probably would have said no to command. Especially if Leonard had survived." Terry worked his jaw in repressed anger. "But once Kan Shimada learned that Dana Sterling might be coming to Tokyo, he asked me to handle things." He grinned at her. "He's eager to meet you."

Dana snorted. "As celebrated war hero or notorious half-breed?"

Terry shrugged. "You'll have to ask him."

The limo sped down a wide highway, populated in large by enormous trucks and fleets of small vans. Though a frequent visitor to near space, Dana hadn't seen much of the planet up close and personal, and so far she was disappointed. Tokyo, said to be Earth's twenty-first-century wonder, looked less like a city than a superhighway system run amok. The residential zones had the makeshift look of slums, and everything in between was a smoke-spewing industrial park. "No wonder the Masters left this place alone," she commented.

Louie and Weston regarded each other and laughed. Louie said, "You're only seeing the roof, Dana."

The city's single tall structure would have been lost among the former milk-carton towers of Monument, though in fact it turned out to be the Shimada Building. Dana thought about Lazlo Zand; it was from here that he had communicated with the Masters, almost two years before the War. Emerging from the limo, she shaded her eyes with her hand and gazed up at the Shimada's airy crown. "That's our destination, I suppose," she said as Terry was climbing from the backseat.

But he shook his head. "We're going the other way." He aimed his thumb at the ground. "Down."

The elevator car had walls of thick glass. After descending several levels through the building itself, the car emerged in Tokyo's vast underground as an exterior elevator affixed to the Shimada's hidden self. Dana realized that they were dropping into an interconnected complex of vast domes—the so-called geo-grid—lit by sunlight and fiber-optic arrays. These housed all that was missing from the surface world: offices, shops, sports complexes, casinos, pedestrian malls, and video gardens. But for all the wonder of it, Dana's awe was corrupted by sadness; for Tokyo was emblematic of what had become of Humankind, driven by three generations of war—global and otherwise—to entomb itself in gloriously appointed bomb shelters.

The elevator stopped well above street level, and Terry led Dana and Louie back into the building. They moved down a carpeted hallway toward a room sealed off by traditional Japanese sliding doors. While they were removing their footwear, a male attendant spoke into his lapel mike and announced their arrival, then Terry escorted them inside, where ten men and one young woman were sitting on the floor around a long, low table. Varying in age from twenty or so to sixty, the men bowed from the waist and spoke to one another in Japanese while Louie and Dana folded themselves into cross-legged postures at the near end of the table. Exquisitely wrought faux wood, the table supported an arrangement of porcelain teapots and cups. Save for the overhead lights, there wasn't a piece of technology to be seen.

"Most revered guests," the silver-haired man at the head of the table said, "you honor us with your visit. Let us hope that this meeting will be the first of many, and that it will lay the groundwork for projects mutually beneficial to our individual and collective causes."

The silver-haired one was Kan Shimada himself. On his right sat his sons, Eiten, Yosuke, and Chosei, and on his left, his most trusted advisors, including Miho Nagata, whose name Dana knew. Closer to her and Louie's end of the table—and dressed way down for the occasion—were two of Shimada's top researchers, Wilfred Gibley and Shi Ling. The young woman's name was Misa Yoshida.

Dana found the first moments of eye contact telling. People who knew anything about her ancestry tended to regard her with a certain wary curiosity; but the penetrating gaze of the Shimadas added respect to the mix, which was something new to her. In a year's time, she seemed to have graduated from half-breed upstart to half-breed war hero. And while she felt gratified, she wished she could have brought along a couple of the Tirolean clones, if only to siphon off the Shimadas' flagrant inquisitiveness. Gibley and Shi Ling, on the other hand, gave her only a moment's gaze before fixing their attention on Louie Nichols, whose whiz-kid reputation had obviously preceded him. As for Misa Yoshida, her dark eyes darted not between Dana and Louie, but between Dana and Terry, who wasn't even seated at the table, but behind Dana, near the sliding doors.

"Mr. Shimada, I, too, hope that something productive can come of our meeting," Dana said when she'd had about all she could take of the silent scrutiny. "But as an emissary of the provisional government and the allied defense forces, I'm obliged to mention that we were hoping President Misui would be included."

Kan Shimada nodded gravely. "Rest assured, Miss Sterling, that everything said here will reach the ears of the president. From our previous dealings—though they may not have been face-to-face—it should be obvious to you, at least, that I am a man of my word."

Shimada was referring to the intercepted communiqué between Lazlo Zand and the Masters. Where the *yakuza* family could have kept the intelligence to itself, Kan Shimada had instead tasked Terry Weston to bring it to the attention of Rolf Emerson, who Terry eventually reached through Dana. As a result, Emerson had been able to use the data to thwart Anatole Leonard's plan to usurp the power of the UEG and crush the Robotech Defense Force. The Shimadas hadn't exactly kept quiet about what they knew—that the Masters' fleet had already arrived in the Solar system—but they had gone about their work of empowering Tokyo without once resorting to blackmail.

"Mr. Shimada, I only needed to hear that President Misui would be apprised of our discussion," Dana said at last. "My adoptive father often said that you would be one of the people on whom Earth's future would rest, and I never doubted that for a moment."

The Shimada *daimyo* inclined his head toward her. "I am deeply saddened by Rolf's death—though all of us should wish for such an honorable ending to our lives." He allowed a moment of silence before asking, "What assistance can Tokyo provide to the beleaguered leaders of the world government and the defense forces?"

Dana switched from a cross-legged position to a kneeling posture. "We know that you have been doing research into something called 'machine mind.' It's rumored that you've discovered a way to bypass the Protoculture interface in controlling mecha. Defense Force command is eager to know if there is any truth to this rumor, and if so, whether you would be willing to share aspects of your research with Robotech Research and Development."

"For the war effort, you mean."

Dana thought for a moment. "Let's say, for the next war effort."

Shimada grinned, showing even, white teeth. "Ah, but here in Tokyo, our sole interest lies in backing the peace effort."

Dana grinned faintly. "Tokyo was certainly within its rights as a sovereign city to exclude itself from the War. But may I respectfully submit that the Masters did not come in peace. If it wasn't for the Macross mounds,

Tokyo might have suffered the same fate that Monument City has."

Shimada showed the palms of manicured hands. "Who can say for certain? Had the Masters been granted access to the mounds, a war might have been averted. Zand and Leonard must have known this. But each, for his own reasons, opted for contest over negotiation. I respectfully submit to you, that, even if it existed in the shadow of the mounds, Tokyo would have responded differently."

"Perhaps," Dana granted. "But it's pretty obvious now that we all exist in the shadow of the Invid. What will Tokyo do when they arrive?"

Shimada's eyes glinted. "Treat them as guests before we brand them as enemies." He paused for effect. "For all anyone knows, the Invid will seek out only those areas where the Flowers of Life are growing in greatest profusion. And should that prove the case, it may be possible to coexist with them. For a time, we shared this planet with the Zentraedi. Why, then, shouldn't we be prepared to share it with the Invid?"

Dana recalled his introductory words to her. *You honor us with your visit. Let us hope that this meeting will be the first of many, and that it will lay the groundwork for projects mutually beneficial to our individual and collective causes.* Was that how Shimada planned to greet the Invid?

He spoke before she could reply. "It is only because the Defense Force will assume that the Invid are our enemies that we are reluctant to share our research with them. We are without ulterior motive in this. You can assure those to whom you answer that we are not like the Southlands' Starchildren cult, readying some dream ship that is meant to deliver us far from Earth and its troubles."

"I'm sure they'll take great comfort in that," Dana said disingenuously. "But make no mistake about it, Mr. Shimada, the Invid are going to disappoint you. True, they probably won't wage war on us like the Zentraedi and the Masters did. They aren't coming to reclaim a hijacked battle fortress or a Protoculture Matrix. They're coming for the Flowers of Life and for the planet on which they've taken root. And they will see us as nothing more than troublesome pests infesting their gardens. They will simply eradicate those of us who resist and enslave the rest. They will construct hives in every part of the world and create orchards and gardens around them. And *we* will be the ones tending those gardens and picking the Flowers, Mr. Shimada. Ask the inhabitants of Karbarra, Spheris, Praxis, Garuda, and countless other worlds. They'll confirm what I'm telling you, because they've lived with it."

Shimada traded baffled glances with his sons. "I know nothing of these places."

"Worlds that were once ruled by the Masters," Dana explained. "But when their empire began to crumble, the Invid rushed in to claim them. This comes direct from the Expeditionary mission, Mr. Shimada. From the commander of the one ship the REF has managed to return home."

"Why wasn't this made public?" Wilfred Gibley asked. "All we heard was that Major Carpenter's ship had been destroyed by the Masters' fleet."

Dana smiled thinly in Gibley's direction. "Whatever my personal indebtedness to you for what you did to Zand, you were hardly considered a Southern Cross ally. Command released only that information that bore directly on the war. I guess it struck Leonard as counter-productive to whip everyone into a frenzy about the Invid while we were still trying to deal with the Masters. Probably the only right choice Leonard ever made."

Shimada steepled his fingers and touched them to his lower lip. "You made no mention of this when you asked if we would be willing to share our technology. Are you proposing some sort of trade—our research for what you know about the Expeditionary mission and the SDF-3?"

Dana glanced at Louie, who gave his head a barely perceptible shake. "I'm not going to lie to you," she said, when she looked back at Shimada. "Major Carpenter was shocked to find the Masters here—in Earthspace. Apparently, it took the SDF-3 several *years* to fold to Tirol, and it took Carpenter's ship almost as many to refold. He thought he'd be returning to the year 2023, not 2032. In other words, his information about the REF is already years out of date. Anything could have happened. The Invid might have been defeated in Tirolspace, or vice versa. We just don't know."

Shimada took a long moment to respond. "What is your personal hunch about the Expeditionary mission?"

Dana was nonplussed. Shimada continued.

"I'm not suggesting that you've had some sort of rev-elation. But, surely, you have a gut feeling about the SDF-3. What with your parents onboard . . ."

Dana was tempted to tell him about her vision, but rejected the idea. Not in this setting, she told herself. Not in her position as emissary. "I'll say this much, Mr. Shimada: I believe with all my heart that the Invid will come to Earth. I wouldn't be here, otherwise. Nor would I have agreed to play this same role with the Zentraedi."

Shimada's sons and advisors muttered and shook their heads. "More surprises from the not-so-guileless Ms. Sterling," Kan's eldest, Chosei, said.

Dana glanced at him. "The Zentraedi have agreed to return the factory satellite to Earth orbit. We're hoping we can use it to ferry some of our disabled warships to what we've determined to be a Sensor Nebula, dispatched by the Invid to search for Flower-rich worlds. Presently, the Nebula is some twenty million miles away. That's why we're interested in knowing what you've learned about mecha control. The reasoning is that the more firepower we can bring to bear on the Nebula, the greater the chances of destroying it. But most of our ships and craft are depleted of Protoculture. We have to find some other way to activate them."

"To resurrect them as agents of death and destruction," Shimada said sadly. "I'm sorry, Ms. Sterling, but I think I prefer them as lifeless rather than animate things."

Dana nodded. "I respect your decision, sir. But there's one more point I need to make: I said that most of our fighters are depleted. But even so, there are hundreds that remain operational. Meaning that the Defense Force is more than capable of *taking* what it wants, when it feels that all attempts at negotiation have failed."

Shimada kept his composure when all about him were losing theirs. "I suspect that you were ordered to say as much, and I appreciate the veil you draped over the Defense Force's threat. Please advise them, in return, that they should feel free to impose their will on us. Without weapons, we would be fools to resist. Therefore, they can come and possess whatever we have—except, of course, our attitude toward peace."

He looked around the table. "You see, Ms. Sterling, we are nondiscriminating toward all would-be invaders: Defense Force or Invid, we will treat them both the same."

CHAPTER
SIX

The Southlands' penchant for tribalism was undoubtedly a legacy of the continent's indigenous peoples: the Inca, the Chibcha, the Moche, the Mapuche, and the countless peoples who inhabited the vast rain forests of the interior. Commentators are quick to assign tribal or cult status to the Church of Recurrent Tragedies, HEARTH, and the Starchildren, but neglect to include the bands of Zentraedi that flourished during the Malcontent Uprisings—the Shroud, the Burrowers, Khyron's Fist, and, of course, the Scavengers—or the scores of "indy" battalions that came into being in the wake of the mass desertions following the Second Robotech War: the Stonemen, the Altiplano Five Hundred, the Pantanal Brigade, and others. Under the heading of Southland factions, one could even, I suppose, include Anatole Leonard's Army of the Southern Cross.

Major Alice Harper Argus (ret.),
Fulcrum: Commentaries on the Second Robotech War

CORDIALITY RETURNED WITH THE END OF THE meeting. Dana and Louie were treated to a grand tour of the Shimada facility, which struck Dana as being closer to what she had read about the complex as it was under Emil Lang than under his chief disciple, Lazlo Zand. Around every corner and crowding every laboratory were robots, curious machines, and computer-created specimens of artificial life. Too, many of the facility's scores of researchers—Asian, for the most part—wore the wide-eyed gaze that had long been associated with

Robotechnology, rather than the "furtive warlock" look that typified the members of the Zand cult, wherein Protoculture was deified.

Kan Shimada and his top *jonin*, Miho Nagata, remained at Dana's side the entire time, drinking in everything she had to say about the Masters and their weapons of destruction, the 15th's reconnaissance of their flagship, and the valiant battles that had been fought on Earth and in near space. Shimada was astonished to learn that a group of Tiroleans had been rescued from the flagship and were currently in protective custody in Monument City.

After three hours of riding elevators, talking to machines, and shaking countless latex-gloved hands, Dana was spent, and was searching for ways to quit the tour. Louie, however—who had spent most of the time talking nonstop with Gibley, Shi Ling, and a cute blond named Strucker—was just getting started. Dana recalled something he'd told her when he was working on his targeting glasses, months before. *I just like machines— period. They expand Human potential, and they never disappoint you if you build 'em right. Somebody with the right know-how—such as myself—could create the ideal society. Unimpeded intellect! Machine logic!*

So Louie decided to remain at the facility while Dana excused herself under the pretense of being exhausted from the transPacific flight. In fact, she was looking forward to spending some personal time with Terry, whom she hadn't seen since long before the start of the War. But when she finally succeeded in locating him—in one of the building's subground-level bars—he was with Misa, who clearly knew Terry as well as, or perhaps better than Dana did.

The three of them retreated to Misa's apartment, in a subterranean luxury high rise only a dome away from the Shimada Building. The apartment was an eccentric combination of traditional Japanese and ultratech, and had a balcony that overlooked a park with a waterfall. Terry was as much at home in the place as he had been in the backseat of the limousine. Misa—who was long-haired, curvaceous, and taller than Dana—wasn't a researcher but some kind of glorified accountant, though how number crunching had earned her a place at the Shimada table was anyone's guess.

The opulence of the apartment discomfited Dana; for the first time since the end of the fighting, she felt uncertain of her place in the world. How could all this exist, she asked herself, in light of what had happened on the other side of the world? The recent past took on a kind of unreality, and for a moment, she could almost convince herself that Rolf, Zor Prime, Jordan Sullivan, and so many others were still alive.

It took several cups of Misa's sake to take the edge off her mood. Pleasantly intoxicated, Dana scarcely batted an eye when Terry informed her that Misa was the person who had inadvertently come into possession of the encrypted data disk that he had turned over to Rolf, and it was the disk that had brought Terry and Misa together. The irony was obvious, in that Terry and Dana had met under similar circumstances during the Giles Academy incident—an intelligence operation mounted by Rolf Emerson, against a Leonard lieutenant named Joseph Petrie.

"We're like blond and brunette bookends for this guy," Dana told Misa between fits of laughter.

As an unsettling dusk descended on the subterranean

city, their talk turned to the state of the world outside the shelter that was Tokyo. Neither Terry nor Misa put much stock in the warnings Dana had voiced about the Invid. To them, it—invasion—couldn't happen a third time. They envisioned a better tomorrow for everyone, and a gradual resurfacing from terror. The thirty-year curse of Macross was ended. The political and military disarray in the Northlands would stabilize, the Southlands would surrender some of its feudal attitudes, Europe and Africa would recover . . . And Tokyo—a kind of inverted Shangri-la—would be there to lead the way into the future.

"Dana, you should think about coming to live here," Misa suggested. "Mr. Shimada would probably appoint you mayor."

Somewhat disarmed by the sake, Dana said, "I'm leaving the planet." It was only when she realized that Misa and Terry were staring at her that she thought to add, "To go to the factory satellite, I mean."

"But when you return," Misa said, looking relieved.

Dana displayed a practiced smile. "When I return. Sure, why not."

On the muddy slopes below Brasília's ruined Esplanada dos Ministerios Brasília, twenty Southern Cross A-JACs deployed in Battloid mode, their quartets of gyro blades slung on their backs like the vanes of a windmill. Above them, dispersed between the spires of debris that had been plasteel and concrete buildings, waited an equal number of Hovertanks and battered Veritechs, several of them also configured in that most Humanlike of fighting modes.

Lieutenant Dewey Tast in Green Tiger One glanced

at his communications console to see the narrow face of
Gavin Murdock resolve on-screen. Murdock was crafted
in one of the Hovers on the Esplanada just now, though
as recently as two months ago he and Tast had been
wingmen during the Emerson-led assault on the Masters' fleet.

"Haven't you got more important things to do, Lieutenant, than to follow a couple of deserters all the way
to the Southlands?"

Tast knew better than to be thrown by Gavin's smile,
which he flashed even when dead serious. "No, Ser-
geant, it's my sad duty to inform you that you're the
only game in town."

"So what game are we playing?"

"It's called 'coming clean,' and here's the way it
goes: First off, you people get together and decide
whether you want to be military or civilian. If you
choose civilian, you surrender the mecha and walk
away without any penalties. If you choose military, then
you get to keep the mecha but you have to follow orders."

"And what's the penalty for choosing military?"

"That's the beauty of it: there isn't any. So, either
way, you win."

"Except for losing the mecha."

"As civilians, you have no right to them."

"Oh, yeah? Then what's the penalty for refusing to
play the game, Lieutenant? A court-martial?"

It was a good question, and Tast had to take a moment to consider it.

Once the crown jewel of the Southlands, Brasília had
endured its own brief Rain of Death during one of the
frequent lulls in the pitched fighting in Monument and

out near the moon. Those lulls had come to be feared by everyone downside, for it was then that the Masters' spade fortresses would ravage whatever landmass happened to be below them at the time. Occasionally they would target a specific place, but more often their energy bursts were unpredictable, scouring uninhabited tracts of forest, or leveling mountaintops, or boiling lakes dry.

Brasília's unlucky day had come four months back. The Masters' preemptive attack hadn't lasted more than five minutes, but in that time, the city—given new life by Anatole Leonard when he had led refugees there from the devastated coast following the original Rain of Death—had been laid to waste. Given that everyone had grown accustomed to living out the lulls in the city's poor excuse for an underground, casualties were comparatively light. But there wasn't a building that hadn't been touched by directed light and sent crumbling to the cobblestone streets. Many believed it was because of Leonard that Brasília had been targeted. But what, then, of Mexico City—also ruined beyond repair—where the Masters' nemesis had never even planted his jackboot?

Brasília, nevertheless, was still home to many of the Southern Cross regulars who had followed Field Marshal Leonard to Monument City after the launch of the SDF-3. And it was to their roots they had returned in the course of the mass desertions that had followed the destruction of Earth's primary fleet and the end of the war.

Gavin Murdock was of those who had returned home.

"I'm still waiting to hear about the penalty for refusing to play, Lieutenant?" he directed over the link to Tast's A-JAC.

Tast decided to try a more down-to-earth approach. "Murdock, what do you plan to do down here?"

"Defend ourselves, brother. 'Cause God knows you people aren't going to do it."

Tast shook his head for the cockpit camera. "Look around you, Gavin. There's nothing left to defend."

Murdock acknowledged the comment with a nod. "Maybe not right here, Lieutenant. But not all of the Southlands looks as bad as this place. HEARTH has got things pretty much under control in the interior and up north."

"Is that what you're planning to do—throw in with those cultists?"

Murdock smiled. "Hey, Lieutenant, those cultists are Earth first, you know what I'm saying? They're not about to fight a war that can't be won. The Invid want a piece of planet? Fine, they can have it, so long as they leave us alone to do our thing. We protect *our* property, *our* land, and nobody else's. You can tell that to General Vincinz and the rest of command. Tell him we're not surrendering the mecha, and that he should think of us as an indy battalion. Civil defense, whatever. But we're not taking orders from anyone. Understood?"

Tast sighed wearily. "You've got, what—fourteen Hovertanks and six Veritechs that can hardly stand on their feet? Have you considered that you're out-gunned?"

"Okay, then. Go ahead and shoot us. Eliminate more of Earth's remaining mecha—and mecha pilots. You know, we're not saying that we won't fight if push comes to shove. We're just saying we get to decide when and how."

Tast muted the communication display and opened up a frequency on the command net that connected him to the Green Tiger commander, Captain Vitti, who was waiting with ten more A-JACs, five miles to the south.

"Did you monitor that, Captain?"

Vitti's face appeared on-screen. "I got it."

"Do we show them what for, or do we starve them out?"

"Neither. Let them be." Vitti gave his head a mournful shake. "And let's just pray that the goddamned Zentraedi on the factory satellite will be more inclined to see reason."

Tast thought he could hear Anatole Leonard rolling over in his grave.

Surrounded on three sides by pianos and synthesizers, Bowie Grant noodled his way through a little-known Lynn-Minmei song entitled, "Screaming Across the Skies." It was late morning and the sun was creeping over the jagged ridge opposite the Emerson cabin, dappling the sloping land with golden light. Bowie loved this hour of the day—and now more than ever. Shortly, the air would warm, and perhaps some of the stiffness would begin to leave his fingers.

He could recall a time when the outbuilding that was his studio behind the cabin had been a sanctuary. Home on leave from any number of military academies, he would retreat to the small wooden structure and play keyboards until his fingers were too cramped to move. But even in those days, when music was everything to him, he knew when he had reached a point of diminishing returns; when sheer exhaustion was undermining the effort he was putting into perfecting some dazzling chord progression or arpeggio. Just now, however, concerns about exhaustion and technique didn't enter the picture; he didn't dare allow himself the luxury of a break, for fear of fomenting mass hysteria among the Tirolean clones.

In fact, the relentlessness of his playing had as much to do with maintaining some semblance of order among the refugees as it did with drowning out the sounds of their anguished cries, baleful moans, and unnerving laughter. What with one of the Hovertanks supplying a couple hours of electricity per day, he had tried running a loop track of samples over the camp's improvised PA system, but the Tiroleans—accustomed to Musica's live compositions on the Cosmic Harp—didn't respond nearly as well to recorded music. Against both the emotional outpourings and the near-constant music, Sean and Angelo had simply taken to wearing earplugs round the clock.

Rescuing the Tiroleans from the Masters' disintegrating flagship hadn't exactly been Dana's idea, but the three campbound members of the 15th ATAC held her responsible just the same. Well before the end of the War, sickened by the fighting, the squadron had rebelled against killing the programmed Bioroid pilots. But it was Dana, to whom Bowie had always looked for support, who had set everything in motion; Dana, who had seen something of herself in the Tiroleans and insisted that they had to be cared for. And now she was off on a mission to the just-returned factory satellite, and Louie was still in Tokyo, and responsibility for the refugees had fallen on Bowie, Sean, Angelo, and a handful of volunteers they had recruited into service.

Though no more accustomed to leadership than the Tiroleans were to individuality, Bowie—as both musician and Musica's mate—had inherited the real burden of their custody, regardless that he hadn't the slightest notion on how to proceed. In the same way that the Protoculture pods aboard the Masters' ships had become contaminated by the Flowers of Life, so, too, had the clones become contaminated by *emotions*.

Of the two hundred plus that had been rescued, sixty had already died; some from wounds sustained during the fighting aboard the flagship, others from disease, and others from heart failure brought on by sensory overload, panic, hypersensitivity—Bowie didn't know what to call it. Phlegmatic under the Masters—Dana had once referred to them as "zombies"—they were nothing less than manic without them, milling within the confines of the Emerson camp like dogs before a fox hunt.

With Monument City deserted, save for the diehards and foragers who had taken up residence in the city's crisped towers, Bowie had given thought to relocating everyone to the lower valley, where they would at least be closer to the crashed assault ships that were supplying food—of a sort—for the clones. But the pale and fragile Tiroleans were as ill suited to travel as their gauzy clothing had been to the Northwest's extremes in temperature. They had been made for life in the climate-controlled interior of the mother ships that had carried them from Tirol, and for nowhere else.

En masse, they seemed to be suffering from dislocation. They longed to return to their previous circumstances: to those inboard cities that resembled Old World Venice without the canals; to their lives of meaningless activity and arranged marriages; to their devices—the bioscanners and reprogrammers—that analyzed and modified their behavior as need be; and to the unquestioned authority of their armed and long-haired Clonemasters.

Perhaps most of all they yearned for the return of the three-in-one mentality the Masters had fashioned for their society, in which each clone was part of a Triumvirate and was incapable of individual effort or action. Bowie often asked himself why the Masters had bothered to create such oblivious creatures; but then he supposed that all would-be-gods—beneficent or corrupt—required applause, and the beings equipped to deliver it ...

Still chording with his right hand, Bowie was giving his left a rest when Musica edged into the studio and gave him a wan smile. She was dressed in mismatched items from Bowie's civilian wardrobe, and her long, dark-green hair was tied in a ponytail. A fresh dressing, courtesy of Sean, covered the scorch she had received on her upper arm during the final fight with Karno and some other clones, but the wound had festered and wasn't healing. In her arms, she cradled the infant they had rescued from oblivion. A boy, the infant was sleeping for a change.

"Are things any better with your people?" Bowie asked while continuing to play.

She shook her head. "Worse, Bowie. Most of them wish they had been included among the aged ones the Masters jettisoned from the flagship. We're ... we're at a *loss*."

The jettisoned ones had died in space, as had the thousands who had inhabited the flagship's five sister ships. And Musica, whose Cosmic Harp melodies gave shape and effect to the mental force with which the Clonemasters controlled the population, wanted to hold herself accountable for every death. Many in the camp were eager to saddle her with the blame, as well.

All because she had come into accidental contact with a brown-skinned Human and fellow musician, one who had infected her with emotions. Thus, Musica had been the first in her biogenetically engineered race to shed tears and to press for an end to the hostilities between Earth and the Masters, and the second to defect, after Zor Prime.

"We have to do something, Bowie," she said, approaching him, almost in trepidation. "If any more of us die—"

"We're doing what we can," he said, interrupting his playing to go to her and hold her. His aching hands smoothed her hair, then he took the infant into his own arms. "We knew it wasn't going to be easy, but we're managing, aren't we?"

She nodded, but her eyes were brimming with tears. "For how much longer? Without the Cosmic Harp, cut off from everything we knew, left only with the memory of so many deaths? I led them into this, Bowie, and now I'm powerless to help them. Half of them wouldn't permit me to help even if I could. Even though I'm grieving as much as they are."

For Octavia, Bowie told himself. One of Musica's Triumvirate sisters, Octavia had been shot by Karno before Sean had stomped the clone flat with the foot of *Bad News.*

As if reading his thoughts, Musica said, "Octavia's dying words to me were that we would still be as one. But I don't *feel* her, Bowie. And if I can't feel her, how am I to give voice to her spirit and songs?" She wept into her hands. "I know that Allegra is going through the same ordeal, and yet she refuses to talk to me. My sister hates me for freeing you from capture, and for leading you to the flagship's control core."

"She doesn't hate you," Bowie said, rocking the infant, who had begun to stir. "You're all struggling with being separated from your brothers and sisters, with standing on your own two feet, as we say. That separation—that distance—must seem like hatred, but—"

"Everyone was so noble and compassionate in the final moments of the War," she said, cutting him off. "But now that the fighting is done, people are reverting to their old ways. The general you so loved—Rolf Emerson—he said that we should be careful not to make the mistakes the Southern Cross and the Masters made; that it was imperative to the future of the planet that our two races learn to live together. But look what has happened already." She glanced at the infant. "The woman, Nova Satori, saved the life of this child, and now she is ready to turn us over to the authorities for 'debriefing.' She is back to being the hardened military officer she was when she tried to take me into the custody of the GMP. And she is but a symptom of an illness that will spread unchecked through your people."

Bowie knew that she was right. He and Musica had had to flee to the Macross mounds to escape Nova. Now the brief time they had spent among the blossoming Flowers of Life was almost a fond memory. He leaned forward and kissed away her tears, the infant pressed between their two bodies. "I promised you that we would be an island of peace in this ocean of misery, and, no matter what comes down, I will do everything I can to make that happen."

Musica sighed disconsolately. "Then return us to Tirol, Bowie," she said, collapsing against his knees. "Take us home."

CHAPTER
SEVEN

The Masters not only were aware of the presence of the factory satellite, but they continued to monitor its whereabouts throughout the War. Of course, it would have been easy enough to target and destroy the facility—as they had a Botoru Battalion warship that was later discovered marooned on a moon of [Saturn]—but the Masters were at that point convinced that the Protoculture Matrix would soon be theirs once more, and they planned to repair, re-energize, and redeploy the factory—along with its contingent of Zentraedi—against the Invid. It's conceivable that the Masters also intended to utilize the factory as a kind of clone creche for thousands of new Zentraedi warriors, which—Imperatived—would then engage the swarm.

A footnote in Zeus Bellow's *The Road to Reflex Point* (apparently based on a remark attributed to Nova Satori, in her intel report on the debriefing of Zor Prime)

APPROACHED FROM SPACE STATION LIBERTY, THE factory satellite, despite its enormity, looked shriveled and desiccated. The factory's secondary pods drooped at the ends of their stalks and, except for a few places, the rose hue of the central radish-shaped body had faded completely. The pallid face of a corpse, Dana thought, rouged by the stroke of a mortician's brush.

She had proceeded directly to Liberty aboard a shuttle launched from Japan's Tanegashima Aerospace Facility, which had seen little use since the start of the war. Then, after several days of briefings, Dana and Marie Crystal had piloted coupled Alpha and Beta Veritechs to the factory, recently returned from its cometary orbit, and in whose veritable shadow Liberty now turned. Newly developed sensors, deflectors, and "sanitiziers" allowed the Legios to avoid and/or destroy bits of debris that could have proved catastrophic to the mecha.

En route, Marie and Dana caught up on developments upside and downside, but spent the better part of the short trip talking about Dennis, who was still on Liberty, awaiting transfer orders; and about Sean, who, along with Bowie and Dante, was safeguarding the Emerson camp's tragically diminishing population of Tiroleans.

As a newborn, Dana had been part of the RDF mission that had captured and returned the factory to Earthspace; but she hadn't been aboard since the death of her three Zentraedi godfathers—Rico, Konda, and Bron—years earlier. Rolf had paid it a visit three years ago in response to the Zentraedis' request for permission to quit Earth orbit. They had planned to act as an early-warning system for the arrival of the Masters, and the plan had called for them to inform the Masters that the grail of their twenty-year journey—the Protoculture Matrix—had left Earth aboard the SDF-3, *to be returned to them*. But, for reasons unknown, the Masters had remained incommunicado with the factory-satellite Zentraedi, the Solar system survivors of Dolza's Grand Fleet.

At the time of Rolf's visit, there had been some four hundred Zentraedi living in gender segregation in coffin-size chambers on level seven of the central body. The vast holds above and below level seven had apparently been sealed off, and the sole functioning gate was the iris access that had been retrofitted into the underbelly of the so-called three-o'clock pod. Rolf had told of meeting with the Zentraedi in compartments blotched with pools of lubricant and strewn with refuse, and of how the once-great race of cloned warriors had come to consider themselves "the doomed."

Fifteen at the time, Dana had experienced a troubling ambivalence over the satellite's departure. On the one hand—and notwithstanding the doomed Zentraedi themselves—she was glad to see the gloomy thing go. But should their suicidal plan succeed, Dana would be left the only Zentraedi—well, half Zentraedi—between Earth and Tirol. Either way, she had hoped never to see the factory again, and now here she was, traveling in Rolf's booster trailings, emissary of a military she abhorred and a government that represented scarcely one-fiftieth of Earth's tormented population.

But if some things never changed, others did. The Earth-tech-capable iris gate in the three-o'clock pod would not open, even after repeated promptings from the coupled Veritechs.

"We could try blasting our way through," Dana said.

"Or 'open sesame,'" Marie suggested.

But in the end, with the Legios anchored to the pod's blanched hull, Dana was forced to go extravehicular and squeeze herself through the gate's manually operated emergency membrane, which itself was barely serviceable.

The transfer tube that connected the pod to the factory's central body opened directly on level seven. But Dana didn't have to go that far. In the docking bay, she was met by a group of about seventy-five haggard Zentraedi, all of them female.

"Par dessu," Dana said in greeting, when she had re-

moved her helmet. "I'm ex-lieutenant Dana Sterling, presently attached to the diplomatic service of the provisional government. I assume that you were informed of the purpose of my visit."

That they had been informed hardly prevented them from staring. But their scrutiny was of an entirely different order than what Dana had been subjected to in Tokyo. The gaunt gaze of the female aliens wasn't emboldened by either curiosity or respect, but by unadulterated incredulity.

"Look closely at the eyes," one of the females said at last—a purple-haired crone with a hooked nose. "You can see the Parino in her."

"It's true," commented another, tall and raven haired. "The Parino Template. No Human seed could smother it."

As a group they stepped closer, surrounding her. "I am called Tay Wav'vir," the first announced. "I knew your . . . your *mother*." It was as if she had to force the word from her throat. "Into many a battle I flew with her. Time and again, into the maw of *kara-brek* flew the Quadrono Battalion. Time and again, into the maw of honorable death." She gestured broadly to her comrades. "Now I am *domillan* here. Speaker, among us. Keeper of the Remaining Days."

"And the males?" Dana asked. "Where are they."

"Dead," the black-haired one supplied. "They refused to eat what little sustenance the factory provides, and so they perished. Of starvation, of grief, of self-pity, of dissolute pride. We are the stronger willed of the self-banished. Waiting without surrender. Honoring *our* imperative, *t'sen-mot* through our stance. The original Imperative has died with the Masters."

"Triumphant T'sentrati!" someone shouted, and throughout the bay the call was echoed in defiant volume.

"Are they truly dead?" Tay Wav'vir asked when the cheer had attenuated. "The Masters?"

They had put the same question to the communications and astrogation techs who had overseen the facility's insertion into stationary orbit. So Dana had brought proof, in the form of news footage of the destruction of the flagship, which she played for them on a laptop-size display screen. When the footage had run, the earlier expressions of wonderment returned to their faces.

Dag, Shaizan, Bowkaz ... dead. It was almost inconceivable.

"You, Daughter of Parino, *you* destroyed them," Tay said. "For all of us."

They saluted, and Dana accepted their salutes, as her mother would have wanted her to. *Triumphant T'sentrati!* The lingering images of her Protoculture-vision had aroused feelings of kinship with the Zentraedi, emotions that were even stronger than what she felt toward the clones. But then, as she began to detail the purpose of her mission, the mood in the docking bay grew somber.

"Yes, we monitored the arrival of the Sensor Nebula," Tay Wav'vir said when Dana was finished. "But this facility isn't capable of carrying your ships there, Daughter of Parino. It has made its last burn. Here it rests to be picked apart by time. A *negrota* souvenir of the war. *Worthless.*"

"The Sensor Nebula is impervious to such an attack, in any case," the raven-haired one added. "The

T'sentrati tried on many occasions to silence the things with the energy of our weapons, but to no avail. The Nebula has dispatched its message and the Invid will come. Reserve your firepower, Daughter of Parino—for the swarm."

Dana checked to be sure that her recording devices were functioning. She had thought as much about the Nebula, but her words alone wouldn't have carried much weight with Southern Cross command. Now command would get to hear the sad truth from the lips of the Invid's archenemies.

"My superiors will be informed," she said.

"Is Emerson among them still?" a yellow-haired one asked. "The Emerson who met with Ilan Tinari before we left Earthspace?"

Dana swung to face her in transparent confusion. Ilan Tinari had been Rolf's companion for a short time when Dana and Bowie were ten or so. "How do you people know Ilan Tinari?"

The Zentraedi female looked to her comrades. "Is it possible she doesn't know?"

Tay Wav'vir stepped in front of Dana. "Ilan Tinari was T'sentrati," she clarified. "It was because of you that she left him—Rolf Emerson. You, Daughter of Parino, were a constant reminder to Ilan of what might have been for the T'sentrati, had Humankind accepted us."

Dana was too stunned to respond. Rolf had never revealed Tinari's ancestry. But, why? Had he feared that Dana would never accept being raised by a Zentraedi other than her mother? Or had he been concerned about awakening too much of the Zentraedi in her?

"Emerson, too, is dead," she managed to say.

Tay Wav'vir nodded soberly. "A pity. He was your guardian, was he not?"

Dana swallowed and found her voice. "He was."

"We wanted to ask a favor of him," Tay's black-haired second said. "Having returned to Earthspace in good faith, we wanted to ask him to provide us with weapons and mecha, so that we might have the joy of soaring into battle against the Invid."

"Carry that message to your superiors, Daughter of Parino," Tay Wav'vir said. "Convince them to treat us as the free beings we are, after so long a time."

Before she and Sterling had set a course for the factory satellite, Marie had recommended that he should check out this communications tech named Rawley, who was stationed in Liberty's forward observation post. *Best entertainment outside the game arcade* was what Marie had said. So Dennis—having decided not to read too much into the miss-you message he had received from Nova Satori, and fed up with the snafus that were interfering with his transfer to ALUCE—had decided to give Rawley a try. But now he was sorry that he had.

"I'm not going to be able to get used to seeing that damn thing, hanging out there like some rotten vegetable," Rawley was saying, referring to the factory, whose ventral surface dominated the view from the post's observation blister. His hands were shaking and his armpits were underscored by large, crescent-shaped sweat stains. "First I thought it looked like some kind of sick Christmas-tree ornament, but now I think it's more like a moldy turnip you find at the back of your fridge.

"I mean, the Invid already have that Nebula to zero in on. And now we've gone and given them a Zentraedi facility, the likes of which they've probably targeted and destroyed in who knows how many other star systems in their search for the Flowers of Life."

Rawley shook his head and propelled two unidentifiable white pills into his mouth, washing them down with a gulp of cold coffee.

"Like my life wasn't miserable enough up here without them positioning that turnip right outside my front window. But do they care one iota about Paul Rawley? Not very likely, not very likely at all."

"Maybe it's time to put in for a transfer," Dennis gamely suggested.

Rawley laughed without merriment. "A transfer? You know where I want to be? In some remote corner of the Southlands where no one can find me. A patch of land with a couple of trees and potable water within walking distance. I'll live on rice and beans, or gather nuts and berries. Hell, I'll live on tree bark, if I have to. Bathe in streams, wear a loincloth, fashion tools out of wood and stone.

"I empathize with the deserters," he continued. "I'd follow suit if they'd let me off this baby's rattle. You'll feel exactly the same, Brown, once you've been here for two or three months and they want to put you on medication because they claim you've been raving, which would ordinarily excuse you from duty or get you a medical discharge but doesn't nowadays because there aren't enough people left aboard who know how to read these screens and interpret data. It's my curse that I can—that I can, even though I'm losing my damn mind! But you try sitting in this seat for a while and see what happens."

Rawley paused for air, and Dennis thought he saw an out, but didn't act quickly enough.

"The Church of Recurrent Tragedies, remember that movement? Reps from that cult used to come to my house in Brasília. What was their solution for keeping the Masters and the Invid from Earth's door? Burn incense, chant, meditate, send money to church headquarters. I think they lost most of their membership after the Malcontent Uprisings. But can you stand there and tell me they were wrong? Can you prove that their tactics *wouldn't* have worked if we'd all gotten behind them?"

Dennis had his mouth open to reply when Rawley continued.

"I, for one, am sorry I didn't join them. I, for one—"

He stopped and stared at his vertical bank display screens, then slammed a hand down on a series of buttons. Howling sirens told Dennis that the station had just been put on full-alert status—for the fifth time in as many days.

"I've got a major bogey in sector six," Rawley shouted into his headset. "Not like anything I've ever seen. Earth vector confirmed!"

What the hell? Dennis thought. It couldn't be a Southern Cross ship out that far. So was it some straggler from the Masters' fleet?

"It's the Invid, Brown," Rawley was muttering. "I'm telling you, it's the Invid . . ."

A burst of static crackled from one of the post's speakers, and everyone in the hold turned to it, as if it were a display screen.

A tense silence held sway for a moment; then the speaker came to life once more.

"This is Colonel Jonathan Wolff of the REF," a calm, resonant voice announced. "I'm sure you people have us on your screens by now, and all I can say is that the view looks great from out here. We want very much to come home, folks, so please advise at your earliest opportunity. We have incredible news to share with you."

CHAPTER EIGHT

Rumors persisted throughout the '30s that groups of Zentraedi or Tiresians had survived the wars and were living on the moon or downside, atop remote mountains or deep within vast tracks of forest. Even now (2065), it is not uncommon to hear tales of travelers who have encountered, in Amazonia, Siberia, or elsewhere, itinerant bands of people purported to resemble [Tirolean] extraterrestrials in appearance or aspect. Yesteryear's Bigfoot and Yeti have given way to today's Zentraedi and Bioroid.

Issac Mendelbrot, *Movers and Shakers: The Heritage of the Second Robotech War*

FROM THAT DISTANCE OUT, EARTH WAS STILL ONLY A smudge of light through the bridge's observation bay; but no matter: it was *their* smudge of light.

Colonel Jonathan Wolff made the toast. "To Earth and to the ship that brought us here." A drink bulb raised in his right hand, he patted the armrest of the command chair with his left. "May each of us get to live the dreams we've been nursing about home."

Everyone on the bridge added voice to the toast; then, when they had all sipped from the bulbs, they tossed them toward a waste bucket someone had thought to bring forward from maintenance. Though there were bottles of Karbarran champagne and ale in the galley, the bulbs contained water. No *real* celebrating until they were safely docked in Earthspace and had assessed the situation there, Wolff had told them.

Wouldn't do to have his crew of three hundred stumbling drunkenly from the ship, as if they had just returned from a party on Tirol. They were REF, after all—Robotech Expeditionary Force—and they planned on demonstrating to the Southern Cross just what a strack outfit they had become.

The ship was a substantially modified Garfish, constructed in Fantomaspace and powered by Reflex drives in combination with Protoculture-fueled spacefold generators. Unofficially designated *The Homeward Bound*, it had launched from the Valivarre system one month earlier, and had forged its way through the Fourth Quadrant by executing a series of transluminal, continuum-bending jumps, or spacefolds.

The ship had performed admirably throughout, except in one area: communication with the SDF-3, in orbit around Tirol, had not been achieved. Burst transmissions had been dispatched through ordinary space nonetheless, in the hope that they would eventually be received. The selfsame glitch had plagued the Ikazuchi Carrier commanded by Major John Carpenter, which had yet to be heard from, though it had left Fantoma more than six months earlier.

The dissimilarity in their sizes, profiles, and signatures notwithstanding, the principal difference between the two ships—known only to Lang and Wolff—was that *The Homeward Bound* was capable of executing a refold for Tirol.

Not that Jonathan Wolff had any such designs. To the contrary, Wolff saw Earth as the final stop in a life odyssey that had taken him not only all over the planet, but to worlds he had never imagined existed. Tirol, Karbarra, Praxis, Garuda, Haydon IV . . . the lot of them inhabited by *beings* he had never imagined existed. But he was through with wandering and with wanderlust. His return would mark a new beginning for himself and for the wife and son he had left behind three years earlier. No more licking the wounds he'd suffered at the hands of Lynn-Minmei; no more disabling himself with drink—not so much as a celebratory goblet of Karbarran champagne for him; and an end to the consuming and ultimately self-destructive hatred he had for T. R. Edwards.

He understood that renewed interspecies warfare was likely to subsume the next year or two of his life. But he knew that he would be able to meet every challenge if he could succeed in reuniting with Catherine and Johnny. If he could succeed in winning their forgiveness for the years of selfishness and abandonment.

He sat straighter in the command chair while his crew busied themselves with duties. *His* crew, he thought. Not bad for a guy who had been a Hovertank commander only four years earlier. Moreover, he stood to receive a healthy promotion for piloting the Garfish home. And how could Catherine fail to be impressed by the sight of a general's star glinting from the crown of his RDF command cap? Oh, there were bound to be heated discussions about his decision to remain in the military. But perhaps she would be inclined to see him in a different light once she realized that he was on the side of peace this time around.

In the breast pocket of his jacket, close to his heart, was a message from Emil Lang, which he had been ordered to hand deliver to Rolf Emerson, of the Earth Defense Force. And included among the contents of that message was Lang's disclosure that Zor had concealed the Protoculture Matrix in the Reflex furnaces of the now-interred SDF-1, a fact to which the Masters should be directed in the event that they threatened war. Even though the possibility of that occurring was still several years off.

"Colonel, I've got an enhancement of that gas cloud," Wolff's science officer reported. "It's approximately one-point-five million kilometers from perihelion of Mars. Coming up on screen five."

Wolff swiveled his chair to the monitor, then sunk down in it as the image resolved.

"Colonel?" the duty officer said in concern.

"An Invid Sensor Nebula," Wolff said when he could. "I had my first look at one in the vicinity of Haydon IV when I was with the Sentinels. It's a kind of Flower of Life detector devised by the Invid Regis. A haze of preorganic molecules imbued with what amounts to sentience."

"But what's one doing here?" a tech asked from her station.

Wolff shook his head. "I don't understand it. Unless—" He glanced at the science officer, Wilks. "—unless the Flowers I occasionally saw in the Southlands have begun to proliferate."

"It's as good an explanation as any," Wilks said. "Lang has always maintained that some of the Zentraedi ships that crashed on Earth may have carried specimens of the Flower. Khyron was said to be addicted to the things."

Wolff ran his fingers through his glossy hair. *Good god,* he asked himself, *was Earth going to have to tangle with the Invid before the Masters even arrived?*

The very thought of the sluglike creatures made his skin crawl. He swung around to face the astrogation console.

"Enhance the opticals you shot of Earth, and run everything through our friend-or-foe library. Screen anything out of the ordinary—at full magnification."

The tech bent to her task, whistling in astonishment a moment later. "Colonel, I'm registering anomalous objects in almost every optical. I'll display them in the order taken."

No sooner had everyone given their attention to the heads-up monitor above the astrogation station than exclamations of shock and anger began to ring out from all sides. The computer enhancements revealed an extensive debris cloud containing fragments of Logans, Veritechs, Hovertanks, and weapons platforms—all interspersed among pieces of Tirolean Hovercraft, Bioroids, and assault ships. One optical showed an asteroid-size hunk that could only have come from a starship of awesome dimension.

And yet, there was the factory satellite, intact if somewhat dispirited looking . . . So just what had happened? Wolff racked his brain for answers. It was obvious that a portion of the Masters' fleet had arrived in Earthspace *ahead* of *The Homeward Bound*. But how was that possible, unless the Tirolean scientist, Cabell, had either been mistaken about the time of the Masters' departure from Tirol, or lying?

"Colonel, Space Station Liberty wouldn't have issued the go-to for our insertion unless things were under control," Wilks suggested.

Wolff glanced at him. "The assumption being that the Masters were defeated?"

Wilks inclined his head to one side. "Their first wave, at least."

Wolff compressed his lips. "Then explain how they managed to complete a twenty-year journey in under fifteen years, without the benefit of fold-capable star ships."

"They knew a shortcut?" someone said, breaking the tension.

Wolff let the laughter continue for a moment, before swiveling his chair to face the communications station. "Lieutenant Mouru, dispatch another burst to Liberty," he ordered, trying to ignore the roiling in his stomach. "And, this time, ask them what year it is."

Any tanker worth his or her horned helmet knew all about Jonathan Wolff: one of the first cadets graduated from the Robotech Academy on Macross Island, defender of Venezuela Sector's Cavern City during the Malcontent Uprisings, commander of the illustrious Wolff Pack. And—what with his slicked-back black hair, pencil-thin moustache, and signature wraparound sunglasses—straight out of central casting. Dana had heard personal anecdotes about Wolff from Rolf, who had known him in the Southlands. Of course, Wolff was legendary among the ATAC, too, all the more so for having ridden to distinction in an ancient Centaur rather than in a modern Hovertank. Said to be dashing, romantic, and quite the charmer, Wolff had been a pinup in Dana's locker throughout her years at the Southern Cross Military Academy.

She and Marie learned about Wolff's extraordinary transmission while they were returning the Legios to Liberty. At the same time, they received orders to re-route for ALUCE Base, which was to be Wolff's point of debarkation.

ALUCE was an acronym for Advanced Lunar Chemical Engineering, and hadn't become a military installation until the final stages of the War. Still undergoing conversion, it was little more than a slope-sided trench of landing-pad alloy fronting a large, circular building—a kind of exclamation point in the center of Hayes Crater, at the northern rim of the Sea of Tranquility.

But, like Tokyo, most of ALUCE was concealed from sight in a ten-level subsurface cylinder that had been inserted into a lava tube. The facility boasted separate areas devoted to power and life support, gravitronics, hydroponics, human services, training, recreation, and living quarters. The base's present though somewhat nominal commander was Major General Desmond Nobutu, a charismatic, square-jawed black man, who had demonstrated his mettle in the near-space mop-up operations that succeeded the destruction of the Masters' fortresses. Regardless, what remained of ALUCE's scientists, engineers, and technicians steadfastly refused to acknowledge Nobutu as their commander, and continued to answer solely to their own chiefs of staff.

A blackout had been imposed on communication with *The Homeward Bound* upon receipt of Wolff's not entirely unexpected follow-up query about the current date. Clearly, he and his crew had been laboring under the same misconception John Carpenter had, in thinking that their spacefold from Tirol had been instantaneous. In Wolff's case, it was still unknown just when he had departed Tirol, but the very nature of the query left no doubt that Lang's latest generation of star ships were not without their problems.

In the week it took *The Homeward Bound* to attain lunar orbit, Dana ran herself through a gamut of emotions concerning its arrival. With news of her parents and the rest of the REF looming on the horizon, she was suddenly forced to consider that her hallucinatory experience aboard the flagship had been tinged with prescience. But did the foreseen arrival of Wolff's ship mean that she should give equal credence to the vision's other elements? Did she, in fact, have a younger sister, who had somehow been able to contact her across the reaches of space-time? The possibility was as unsettling as the vision itself; and, because of it, she had scarcely managed more than a few hours of sleep each night.

Driven by a sense that everything she said or did from that point forward would have wide-ranging consequences, she had decided not to reveal what the Zentraedi had told her about the Sensor Nebula. Defense Force command was going to press hard to enlist Wolff's aid in launching a strike against the intelligence-gathering cloud, but Dana planned to say nothing until she had heard Wolff out.

By the time the colonel and his chief crew members arrived at ALUCE, dozens of officers and officials were waiting for them. But despite the brave smiles with which the crew of *The Homeward Bound* greeted their ovation, it was apparent from their awkward movements that they were unstuck in time; that the revelation about the chronological disparity had shaken them to their very cores.

Wolff most of all, by the look of him.

Everyone assembled in a small amphitheater on

ALUCE level two, which was being forced on that occasion to accommodate twice the number of people it had been designed for. Wolff and some of his officers shared the amphitheater's focal point, along with generals Vincinz and Aldershot, representing the Southern Cross and the GMP, respectively; senators Constanza, Grass, and Harding; and several scientists from ALUCE and downside.

Vincinz's adjutant, a burly major named Stamp, furnished *The Homeward Bound* contingent with a summary of the salient events of the past twelve years, commencing with the rise to power of Anatole Leonard and the Army of the Southern Cross. The war itself was given relatively short shrift, though Stamp did touch on several key incidents, including the arrival of Carpenter's ship, the capture and defection of Zor Prime, and the attack on Monument City and the Macross mounds, in which Leonard, Moran, Zand, Emerson, and thousands of others had died, and in which the Protoculture Matrix had been destroyed.

Then, plainly disturbed by all that he had absorbed, Jonathan Wolff stepped to the podium and recounted the most incredible tale.

As early as 2012—thanks to Zentraedi commander Breetai and his dwarfish advisor, Exedore—Humankind had been apprised of the existence of a myriad of intelligent races inhabiting the Milky Way galaxy. More recently, John Carpenter had supplied information about the Sentinels and their campaign to liberate the Invid-held worlds of Tirol's local group; the resizing of the Zentraedi and the renewal of mining operations on Fantoma; and about the schism that had split the Expeditionary Force.

But unlike Carpenter, Wolff was able to supply *first-hand* accounts of the battle on Karbarra, the destruction of Praxis, and the strange reversals that had occurred on both Haydon IV and Tirol. He told of the assassination of an Invid simulagent, for which he himself had been blamed; and of the events that had led to his hijacking a star ship. And he told of the Sentinels' struggle to reverse a curse that had gripped the planet Peryton; and of the trial in which T. R. Edwards had been unmasked as a traitor. Finally, almost as an afterthought, he mentioned the child born to Max and Miriya Sterling on Haydon IV ...

But Wolff's was a maddeningly unfinished tale, for he had left Tirol shortly after Edwards and his Ghost Squadron had launched for Optera in order to join forces with the Invid Regis, and almost *five years* had passed since then. Consequently, there was no telling how the events in Tirolspace had played out, though the continued absence of the SDF-3 seemed to indicate that something untoward had occurred.

When everyone in the auditorium had had several minutes to grapple with the implications of Wolff's account, General Aldershot asked him straight-out if the ship was fold capable.

Dana was seated close enough to the podium to take note of Wolff's momentary hesitation.

"Our aim was simply to come home," Wolff finally said.

"But is it worthy for near-space travel?" General Vincinz asked.

Wolff nodded. "Within limits. But for what purpose?"

"To destroy the Sensor Nebula—which you yourself have indicated is a harbinger of the Invid."

Wolff studied the Southern Cross commander in chief for a moment. "We could try, I suppose."

"Try?" Vincinz sneered. "It has been proposed, Colonel, that the detonation of several thermonuclear warheads should suffice to disperse the cloud."

"And if the cloud's already done its dirty work?" Wolff said.

One of ALUCE's astrophysicists cleared his throat in a meaningful way. "We're going on the assumption that the Nebula also serves as a biological beacon—a kind of homing device for the swarm. Unless, of course, you can present us with evidence to the contrary."

"No, I can't. As far as I know, the Nebulas contain some biological components, invested with a kind of raw Protoculture of the Regis's devising. Dr. Lang once characterized them as 'entropic,' but I'm not sure why." Wolff's frown faded, and in its place surfaced a look of heroic readiness. "I'd like to volunteer the services of myself and my crew to carry out the mission."

Senator Constanza traded significant glances with his peers while separate conversations broke out throughout the hall.

"We are deeply indebted to Colonel Wolff for the information he has provided, and for his offer to effect the destruction of the Invid Sensor Nebula," Constanza said when the amphitheater had quieted. "However, I must caution General Vincinz that he is not in a position to assign the mission to Colonel Wolff or, indeed, to any other officer."

Vincinz came slowly to his feet to glare at Constanza. "Perhaps you should explain yourself, Senator."

Constanza leaned back in his chair, almost as casually as he might have done in full-standard gravity. "In

2019, the Robotech Expeditionary Force was placed at the disposal of the United Earth Government, as represented by the members of the Plenipotentiary Council. And since we"—he gestured to his fellow senators—"are the vestiges of the UEG, it follows that Colonel Wolff—if he will excuse the phrase—is ours to command, with or without his ship, which I hearby place in the custody of the Global Military Police, until such time as it is deemed appropriate to execute a strike against the Nebula."

Vincinz's face grew flushed. "You seem to be forgetting that the *Southern Cross* bears responsibility for defending the planet, Constanza."

The senator was unmoved. "The leaders of the Southern Cross apparat are dead, or have been judged guilty of treason. T. R. Edwards—if he hasn't been executed—is probably imprisoned on some forlorn moon. And had they lived, Supreme Commander Leonard and Chairman Moran would surely be facing similar fates. What's more, 80 percent of the Southern Cross's ground-based forces have deserted, whereas 70 percent of General Aldershot's GMP forces have remained devoted to duty. Add to this the fact that two REF contingents have now returned to Earth, and only one conclusion can be drawn: the barbarous reign of Anatole Leonard is finally ended, *General* Vincinz."

CHAPTER NINE

We desperately wanted to host [Wolff's] parade, but Constanza and his bunch wouldn't hear of it. Manhattan was just too far removed from all that Rocky Mountain action: Macross, Monument, Denver, and the rest. More importantly, as a city, we were still on the comeback trail, with too few residents and a dearth of mecha to give the parade the proper military touch. In retrospect, though, Constanza made the right choice. The parade would certainly have resulted in increased immigration, which would have only put more people in Manhattan when the Invid Regis arrived, and left more corpses in the streets after she doused us with death. You have to grant one thing, however: Despite the attacks by Dolza, the Masters, and the Regis, despite the staggering number of fatalities over the decades, the city itself never fell. The place was built to last.

Mayor Mario Peebles, as quoted in Xandu Reem's
A Stranger at Home: A Biography of Scott Bernard

"THE MOLE WE PLACED WITHIN THE GLOBAL Military Police reports that another warship has returned from Tirol," Kan Shimada announced to the table, between forkfuls of buttery-smooth steak. "The ship is smaller than the one that appeared last year, but well armed, and is under the command of a Colonel Jonathan Wolff, who was apparently a member of the so-called Sentinels. Since news of Wolff's arrival is to be made public next week, we have only until then to exploit this unexpected, and potentially inauspicious, development."

The name of the restaurant was Tokonama. Situated

six levels below Shinjuku Station and commanding a view of the entire Shinjuku dome, it was one of many Family-owned and operated establishments in the geo-grid. But the Tokonama was Kan Shimada's preference when he was in the mood for pre-Rain decadence; for the restaurant was renowned for its *kobe* beef, New Zealand wines, and exquisite desserts, which were often served in fanciful, edible containers.

Misa knew from previous experience that Kan Shimada only indulged in pre-Rain fare when he had matters of a serious nature to discuss, and so she had come prepared to do more listening than eating. Terry Weston accompanied her, still downside on leave, though only that morning he had received orders to return to ALUCE on the next shuttle out of Tanegashima. They had spent a wonderful week together, and had even made love—once Misa had assured herself that Terry's feelings for Dana Sterling hadn't been rekindled by her brief visit to Tokyo.

The silk-and-linen corporate crowd that normally patronized the Tokonama had been told to keep away, and on arriving at the restaurant, Misa and Terry had noticed more than the usual number of Family enforcers and *kumi-cho* about, seeing to crowd control and security. That Kan Shimada was the city's undisputed *oyabun* didn't insure against people who wished him ill.

"A briefing was held at ALUCE, during which it was proposed that Wolff's ship be used against the Invid Sensor Nebula, of which Dana Sterling spoke," Kan Shimada continued. "The feasibility of disabling the cloud is still under discussion, but that dispute is irrelevant to my concerns about the ship itself."

Shimada took a sip of wine and patted his full lips

with a cloth napkin. Seated at the opposite end of the table, Misa leaned slightly to one side, the better to see Shimada around an enamel vase full of freshly cut flowers.

"To come directly to the point, this ship poses a risk to our plans to open negotiations with the Invid. The waning power base of the Southern Cross aside, I am unclear as to the intentions of the surviving members of the provisional government. Were it not for the loyalty of the Global Military Police, the UEG could be toppled and we could be done once and for all with this pretense of a central bureaucracy. But as things stand, we are forced to deal with the likelihood of a refurbished government. And while Constanza and the others *appear* to be more levelheaded than their predecessors, we have no guarantee that they won't engage the Invid as Leonard did the Masters—especially now that Wolff's ship has provided them with the capacity to do so."

Shimada's youngest son, Yosuke, refilled his father's glass with red wine. Kan took a sip and set the glass aside. "I see no harm in allowing Wolff—or whomever commands the ship—to carry out the Sensor Nebula mission. But I believe it will be in our best interests to make certain that the ship disappears soon afterward."

Miho Nagata's deep voice broke the silence that fell over the table. "Sabotage?" he said.

Shimada rocked his head from side to side. "I'm not sure we need to be thinking along those lines just yet. There are many groups that would leap at the chance of commandeering that ship—the chiefs of staff of the presently disaffected Southern Cross, to name but one."

"I would add the Zentraedi to the list," Miho said.

"Our mole reports that the factory satellite is effectively dead in space."

"Yes, they should also be considered."

"What about the Starchildren?" Chosei offered.

Kan stroked his chin. For ten years, the Southlands cult had been seeking a means of moving its membership offworld. "Certainly."

"Do we know if the ship can fold?" Eiten asked.

"Wolff asserts that it can't," his father said. "But can Wolff be taken at his word? For all we know, he was dispatched by the REF to evaluate conditions in Earthspace and report back to Tirol. But let us assume for the moment that Wolff is telling the truth. Is there no way of reconditioning the ship's existing drives to render them foldworthy?"

Shimada directed the question to Gibley and his team, who were actually sporting *suits*—though of a late-twentieth-century cut.

"Louie Nichols, who was here with Dana Sterling, alerted us to several encouraging avenues of research," Gibley said. "But first we'd need to have a look at the ship's Reflex furnaces and spacefold generators."

Shi Ling glanced at Gibley and picked up where he left off. "Nichols is interested in investigating something he calls 'Syncron technology,' which involves the generation of a singularity effect. The procedure was successfully employed during the war, and Nichols is of the opinion that, properly tamed, the effect can be employed to execute an instantaneous spacefold."

Shimada adopted a thoughtful pose. "Where is Nichols now?"

"In the Northlands," Gibley told him. "In a refugee

camp just outside Monument City, staffed by the former members of the Sterling's 15th ATAC squadron."

Shimada looked at Miho Nagata. "Make contact with Nichols. Tell him that we are reconsidering the UEG's request for an assessment of our research into machine mind. Suggest to Nichols that we would like him to act as liaison between our technical teams and theirs, and gently hint that we have learned about the arrival of a star ship. Set the stage for eventual terms that would allow us to inspect Wolff's ship as a prerequisite to any bargain involving our findings."

"*Hai,*" Miho said, bowing slightly.

Shimada's eyes roamed the table. "In the meantime, we must begin to rouse a craving for Wolff's ship, wherever possible." His eyes came to rest on Misa and Terry. "Have either of you ever had any dealings with the Starchildren?"

"Indirectly, sir," Weston said. "I met Kaaren Napperson—the cult's founder—about eight years ago, in Monument City."

Shimada nodded. "We have an operative among them. She will acquaint you with all you need to know about the Starchildren. Then I want you and Misa to undertake a trip to their colony in the Southlands." His determined gaze favored Terry. "I will see to it that your leave is extended."

Terry inclined his head.

"I suspect that the Starchildren will take a great interest in Wolff's ship. And even more in the fact that we could be convinced to fund an operation that would deliver the ship into their hands."

* * *

Shaved and showered in the hotel suite the UEG had provided for him in Denver, Jonathan Wolff gave half an ear to the TV news coverage of the parade in which he and his crew had been honored.

"Wolff performed heroically with the Sentinels," a male commentator was saying, "on one occasion rescuing Admirals Rick Hunter and Lisa Hayes Hunter in a star ship he skyjacked from Tirol; and on another, agreeing to stand trial for crimes he didn't commit, just to see that General T. R. Edwards was brought to justice."

An attractive, fair-haired female commentator came on-screen. "The devilishly handsome commander of *The Homeward Bound* reports that the Invid swarm have been routed from every planet on which they've set foot—or is that pseudopod?—and that the Earth will be no exception."

"Should the Invid come, the Sentinels will be hot on their trail; is that the idea, Leana?"

Leana smiled for the camera. "That seems to be the long and short of it, Roger. So a word for you Invid out there, if you're listening: Jonathan Wolff is home, and he's going to be out there gunning for you . . ."

Dismayed by the portrait being painted of him, Wolff silenced the TV with a voice command. He had anticipated being swallowed up by the UEG's propaganda machine, but he hadn't expected to be recast as a savior. He supposed, to some extent, that the hero bit came with the territory, but that was no excuse for portraying the Invid as a swarm of killer bees.

With the collapse of the Southern Cross, his promotion to general seemed all but assured. The recommendations would have to come from General Aldershot and his command staff, of course, but given that they had all been die-hard Robotechs even before Global Military Police, he felt certain that he could count on their support. However, though they scarcely mattered in the big picture, he had no such faith in the members of the UEG. Just who was Constanza trying to kid, anyway, acting as if he and a handful of senators had run of the planet, when Japan, China, the Southlands, and most of Europe wouldn't have anything to do with them?

Wolff wasn't entirely clear himself on his reasons for withholding information about the fold capability of the ship. When the question had been put to him, his survival instincts had taken over. It had struck him at the time that someone was going to have to return to Tirol to apprise Reinhardt, Lang, and the Hunters about the war with the Masters, and about the space-time disparities that plagued the Tirol-made ships. He had lied as a means of retaining some control over *when* that mission would be launched. As to who would command it, he was undecided.

Wolff moved from the bathroom to the bedroom, where his uniform was laid out. As he began to dress, he thought about Catherine and Johnny, who were due to arrive at any moment. He wondered if the flight from Albuquerque had carried the televised parade, and whether they had caught any of it.

While buttoning his shirt, he realized that his hand was shaking, and he glanced at the suite's wet bar, with its tidy assortment of bottled brandies and liquors. Just one drink, he started to tell himself; then he came to his senses.

It was never *one* drink.

Regarding himself in the full-length mirror, he couldn't accept that twelve years had passed since he last saw them. Had *The Homeward Bound*, and the SDF-3 before that, entered some new space where time didn't exist? Otherwise, shouldn't his body betray the years? The crew and the members of the Wolff Pack felt as discombobulated as he did, though most of them hadn't left family behind on Earth. Hunter had chosen them for precisely that reason.

And yet, in spite of everything, it was wondrous to re-experience Earth after the dizzying artificiality of Haydon IV and the lunar sterility of Tirol. Too bad about Monument City—though he had never really warmed to the place. He did, however, want to visit Albuquerque and Cavern City, even if the latter had been overrun by some cult that called itself the Heal Earth Hajj.

But all that would have to wait until he got his land legs. Physicians at ALUCE had pronounced him to be in good health, but he didn't feel 100 percent. In fact, the closest he'd come to feeling shipshape was on the shuttle trip down the well, during which he had gotten to know Max and Miriya Sterling's perky 18-year-old daughter, Dana, who had proved herself to be as able a warrior as her parents. Wolff remembered her as the girl who had carried the flowers at the Hunters' factory-satellite wedding, ages ago, but, oh my, how she had grown and filled out! Talking with her, he could almost forget that she was half Zentraedi—not that he held that against her, in any case. Why, even during the Malcontent Uprisings, some of his best friends had been aliens.

He was thinking of Dana when the door chime sounded, and his heart began to race. Giving a final downward tug to his tunic, he hurried to the door and threw it open, grinning like a kid, even through his initial shock. Catherine seemed as little changed by the years as he was, but Johnny . . . Where was the teenager Wolff had planned to pull into an embrace and clap on the back? Who was this sullen-looking *man* who had his father's black hair and his mother's sculpted features?

Catherine permitted herself to be hugged, but she returned none of the warmth he exuded. "You look wonderful," he said, stepping back awkwardly. And indeed she did: the mounds of red hair, the noble forehead and cleft chin . . . She was heavier by ten pounds, he guessed, and her eyes were encased in a network of fine lines that hadn't been there twelve years ago, but she was every bit as striking as she had been on the day they'd met.

Johnny stuck out his hand and said, "Hello, Colonel," in a tone that somehow blended hostility with sadness.

Wolff ushered them into the suite, took their bags, and offered them drinks from the wet bar, which they declined. Catherine sat on the couch, taking in the room. Johnny remained standing, with his hands thrust deeply into his trouser's pockets and his eyes lowered. The suite's air-conditioner hummed loudly.

"I thought long and hard about not coming," Catherine said after a moment. "But I decided it would be better this way. We were never good on the phone."

Wolff sat down opposite her, resisting an urge to reach for her hands. "I'm glad you came. I would have gone to Albuquerque, but I'm scheduled for dozens of briefings."

"The price of glory," Johnny muttered.

Wolff glanced at him. "I didn't apply for the position as hero," he said, more strongly than he meant to.

"What do you want with us, Jonathan?" Catherine said quickly. She reached for her purse, lifted a cigarette from a flat case, and lighted it. "We watched the parade. We heard several news accounts of your exploits on Tirol and other places. We're very happy for you. You have exactly the life you dreamed of having."

Wolff watched her exhale a cloud of smoke; an athlete, she had despised cigarettes. "What I did on Tirol, I had to do. But I came home because I wanted to. Because I missed you—both of you—and I want to apologize for leaving."

Catherine's green eyes narrowed. "Why are you apologizing? You made a choice, Jonathan. You knew full well what you were doing."

He compressed his lips. "I made the wrong choice. I see that now."

She laughed her mouth empty of smoke. "You must be kidding. You think you can just come blasting back into our lives after twelve years? I'm sorry, Jonathan, but I don't see that there's anything left between us."

"There're my feelings. Or don't they matter?"

"Please," she said nastily. "Are you telling me that you're resigning from the REF?"

"Well, not right away," he said. "But after we resolve our differences with the Invid, then, yes, I'm prepared to resign, if that's what it'll take."

She shook her head in self-amusement. "You'll never be happy as a civilian. Look what happened when we moved to Monument City. You lasted four months before you applied for a transfer to the REF, because you couldn't stand the boredom of a desk job. And it's a good thing you did ship with the SDF-3, because the Masters took a long time getting here, Jonathan, and you would have been chomping at the bit."

"That's done with," he snapped. "If it wasn't for the Invid—"

"You'd follow me to Albuquerque and play the happy husband?" She stubbed out the cigarette. "Has it occurred to you that I might have a life of my own now? What do you think I've been doing all these years—watching the stars for your return? Oh, I did, for a time. But I had a son to raise, and to send through school, and to keep out of the hands of the Southern Cross, and to keep safe from the Masters . . ."

Her voice began to break up, and Johnny laid a comforting hand on her shoulder, scowling at Wolff the whole while.

"And what about our *age* difference?" she continued after a moment. "You don't think that's going to be a problem? Because, you see, I heard from the wife of one of John Carpenter's bridge officers that you'd taken a liking to younger women."

Wolff swallowed. "I'm telling you, all that's behind me."

She stared at him. "Lynn-Minmei is out of your system, huh? Just a mad infatuation?"

"I came home for you, goddamnit."

Her look was pitying. "Well, then, I'm afraid you made another wrong choice."

"We suffered our eighty-first fatality just last night," Bowie told Dana, pacing nervously as he spoke.

"From disease?" she asked.

He stopped to glance at her. "Sure, if you can call homesickness a disease."

They were in the wood-paneled den of the cabin, a room they had grown up in and was layered in memories. Angelo was there as well, while Sean and Louie were in Monument, securing supplies. Dana had only returned to the compound that morning, after more than a week of debriefing in Denver regarding her visits to Tokyo and the factory satellite. She had been there for the parade, though she hadn't had a chance to speak with Wolff afterward. She had found herself thinking about him, though, ever since their long conversation aboard the shuttle from ALUCE. Jonathan really was the stuff heroes were made of, much more comfortable with the role than she recalled her father being. Even so, it hadn't been the easiest conversation to sustain. She had talked to Wolff—her pinup—so often in her thoughts, that she could scarcely bring herself to meet his gaze.

"The upper-forty is getting to be a regular boot hill, Dana," Angelo said.

Bowie nodded solemnly. His dark-brown face looked drawn. "We have to do something. I've been playing for them ten hours a day and it isn't making a difference."

"What's Musica have to say about all this?" Dana asked him.

"They want to go home, Dana, and that's all there really is to say. It's like we rescued them from the flagship just so that they could die here."

Dana thought about the Zentraedi females in the factory satellite, about whom the same thing could be said. When she had brought up the idea of arming them in advance of an Invid invasion, Aldershot, Fredericks, and Nova Satori had practically laughed in her face—though they had tentatively agreed to have the iris gate repaired. In the wake of the unexpected arrival of *The Homeward Bound*, the depleted factory had lost any real significance. And unless Dana disclosed what the Zentraedi had said about the futility of attacking the Nebula, Aldershot and the members of Constanza's oversight committee would soon be turning their attention to the selection of a commander to head up that mission.

"We've got some serious decisions to make, Lieutenant," Angelo was saying.

She frowned at him. "Don't call me that."

Angelo snorted. "Well, for someone who claims to have resigned from the military, you sure seem to be taking on a lot of assignments. If you don't mind my saying so."

"I do mind your saying so, Angelo. I'm only trying to prevent us from making the same mistakes we made with the Masters."

"Is Colonel Wolff's ship going to be able to take out the Nebula?" Bowie said.

Dana considered her response, then shook her head and recounted what Tay Wav'vir had told her. Long before she was through, Angelo was bristling.

"Why are you keeping this from General Aldershot?" he demanded. "What, you'd rather see the Defense Force expend firepower than dash their hopes of throwing the Invid off track?"

Dana kept shaking her head. "I'm not sure I can answer that, Angelo. Aldershot probably isn't going to accept the word of a couple of atavistic Zentraedi, anyway. But if he does, and the mission is scrubbed . . ." She looked at Angelo. "I suppose it is a matter of not dashing their hopes."

Angelo smiled wryly. "Even though you don't believe the Nebula can be destroyed."

"Right. Even though I don't believe it."

Sean and Louie returned just then, each of them carrying crates of emergency rations. Dana hadn't seen Louie since the meeting with the Shimadas, and by the look of him—in coveralls, goggles, and jester cap— some of Tokyo had worn off on him.

"Guess who I was just talking to?" Louie said after giving her a stiff hug. "Miho Nagata."

"One of Kan Shimada's captains or bosses or whatever they call themselves," Dana told Bowie and Angelo. "What did he want?"

Louie grinned broadly. "Seems that the Shimadas might be willing to let us in on what his scientists have been up to these past couple of years, after all."

Dana's eyes widened in surprise. "Louie, that's *great* news!"

"It is. But there's an 'if' attached to the offer. Miho hinted that we'll get to evaluate their research *if* the powers that be can be persuaded to allow Gibley and his team access to the fold core of Wolff's ship."

"Why?"

"To determine whether the fold generators can be revitalized."

"Is that possible?" Angelo asked.

"Gibley and I think so."

"Gibley and *you*?"

Louie crossed his arms over his narrow chest. "That's

the other part of it. The Shimadas want me to come to work for them."

"What kind of crap is this?" Angelo said angrily. "You can't leave us now. We need you here."

Dana stepped between them. "Yes, he can, Angelo. In fact, he has to." She looked over her shoulder at Louie. "I saw it that first day in Tokyo. You belong with them. You'll make a difference there."

Louie loosed a relieved exhale. "Thanks, Dana. But what about the terms of Shimada's deal? Do Gibley and I have a shot at examining that ship?"

Dana took her lower lip between her teeth. "All I can do is propose it to Aldershot and the members of the oversight committee. But I don't see how they could refuse if there's even an outside chance of revitalizing the fold generators. Establishing contact with the SDF-3 has to take precedence over everything else. We've got to find out what happened on Tirol, and the REF has to be told what's happened here."

"Dana, I just had a crazy thought," Bowie said a moment later. "Let's say Louie and this Gibley succeed, and the ship is programmed to return to Tirol. How about our making sure that the Tiroleans are part of the cargo?"

Dana beamed at him. "We'll do it—even if it means taking everyone upside ourselves."

Wolff and Carpenter were cut from different cloth. From the start, Wolff had been out to make a name for himself, in Cavern City during the Uprisings, and later as the flamboyant commander of the Wolff Pack. Carpenter, on the other hand, while a respected officer, had the kind of self-effacing, quiet strength that didn't draw attention to itself. Brought together at the start of the Third Robotech War, they would make a good team for a time, but suffer an eventual falling out, from which their relationship would never recover. A loner who never married, Carpenter—who would survive the Invid—claimed that he might have tempered his judgment of Wolff had he understood what Wolff was going through with his wife and son. But he never absolved Wolff for absenting himself from Nobutu's attack on Reflex Point, for the sake of a "harebrained" rescue attempt. If there was some measure of hero worship on Carpenter's part before the Invid Invasion, there was nothing but disillusionment afterward.

Mizner, *Rakes and Rogues:
The True Story of the SDF-3 Expeditionary Mission*

"**W**OLFF!"

"Hello, Carpenter. Good to see you again." Wolff extended his hand, but Carpenter brushed it aside and pulled him into an embarrassingly lengthy embrace. Fortunately it was just the two of them in the subterranean briefing room of the GMP's new headquarters, a hundred miles south of Denver. Nova Satori, the raven-haired deputy director of intelligence, had arranged for them to have a couple of minutes together before the briefing began.

"I can't believe you're here," Carpenter was saying,

with a tight grip on Wolff's upper arms. "I was beginning to think I'd never see any of you again."

Wolff eased out of Carpenter's hold and grinned. "Lang thought the same about you. But I had a sense you'd made it home. It was a courageous act, Major—agreeing to pilot that retrofitted Ikazuchi."

Carpenter's dark eyes shifted. "Some of what we did might have been courageous. But some of it was just plain stupid."

Wolff assumed that he was referring to his frontal attack on the Masters' flagship. "Not that it matters, I suppose, but I would have done the same thing."

Carpenter showed him an intent look. "It does matter, Wolff. It matters a great deal."

They hadn't known each other well, either before the launch of the SDF-3 or on Tirol. When the Hunters, the Grants, the Sterlings, Wolff, and so many others had agreed to throw in with the aliens who comprised the Sentinels, Carpenter—at Lang's behest—had volunteered to remain in Tirolspace, as a precaution against possible acts of sedition by T. R. Edwards and his Ghost Squadron.

Carpenter's elation notwithstanding, the real reunion was taking place elsewhere on the GMP's base, between members of Carpenter's crew and those of Wolff's who had once been attached to Carpenter's command. Those dozen or so would have been home all the sooner had they not assisted in the hijacking Lang and Wolff had staged. That heroic act had provided the Sentinels with a replacement ship for the *Farrago*, which had been lost to the Invid above Praxis.

Carpenter had suffered a nervous breakdown after his fiery return to Earth, and had spent the final months of the War with friends in Portland, coming to terms with the destruction of his ship and the displacement of ten years of his life. As a consequence of that breakdown and the loss of the data stored in the ship's computer, much of what he told Leonard's staff and the GMP had met with unvarnished skepticism. That Wolff and *The Homeward Bound* had provided corroboration for Carpenter's earlier claims about the Invid and the Sentinels figured strongly in Carpenter's delight in seeing him.

"Wolff, I've got a million questions," he started to say.

But Wolff held up his hands. "I don't have the answers, Major. I'm sure you've read the reports. In the scheme of things, we launched right behind you. And that was five years ago."

Carpenter fell silent and wearily lowered himself into a chair at the foot of the briefing room's plastic laminate table. "I still can't get used to this," he said after a moment. "When I saw my friends in Portland, it came home to me. Ten years . . . People see me and they say how terrific I look, and I want to grab them by their shirtfronts and tell them that it feels more like I *lost* ten years than gained them. Forget what the stress has done to me." He looked up at Wolff. "How are you and your people handling things? You left a wife and kid back home, didn't you?"

Wolff concealed his pain. By the time Catherine and Johnny had left the hotel suite, he had at least gotten her to *consider* giving him a second chance, but he was hardly encouraged. Johnny had remained brooding throughout, and Wolff suspected that Catherine's apparent thaw was nothing more than an attempt to bring their reunion to a quick conclusion. When he spoke of visiting them in Albuquerque, Catherine had told him not to rush, because she didn't want to feel pressured. *You've made another wrong choice . . .* He was tempted to admit to Carpenter how it had crushed him to hear her say that; how it had undermined the grandiose plan he had outlined for the future. But he held back.

"Some of us are taking it better than others" was what he finally said.

Carpenter nodded knowingly.

"What about your people, Major? Are they still a unit?"

Carpenter took a breath. "Not so you'd notice. More than a third have resigned from service. I refuse to see it as desertion—not after what they've been through. I know where some of them are. Hell, there's a group of them living not too far from here in the husk of a depleted Garfish. Veterans of the war against the Zentraedi. So who am I to tell them they have to fight the Invid? All of us went a little crazy, I guess. Don't be too surprised if the same thing takes hold of your crew, Colonel."

"I'll keep that in mind."

Carpenter regarded Wolff for a moment, formulating his thoughts about something. "The ship, Colonel—it can't refold?"

Wolff shrugged. "Maybe someday."

"I only mention it because, well, I'd be honored to have a place on your crew—in the event you were thinking about taking her back to Tirol, I mean."

"For the moment, that ship isn't going any further than the Sensor Nebula," Wolff said firmly. "But I'd be glad to have you aboard on that mission, if it falls to me."

"Can the Nebula be destroyed? You've had more experience with those things than I've had—and with the Invid."

Wolff took a breath. "It can't hurt to try."

The center-pull doors opened just then, and Nova entered the room, trailed by Dana Sterling, Alan Fredericks—now a colonel—and several members of the UEG's oversight committee. Accompanying them was a lantern-jawed civilian, wearing outsize, tinted goggles.

"I don't trust that one," Carpenter whispered of Nova as Wolff was dropping himself into the adjacent seat. "She's the one who debriefed me after we tangled with the Masters." He appended a choice epithet.

"Something to report, Major?" Nova asked suddenly, regarding him from the far end of the table.

"Nothing of relevance, ma'am."

"Then I strongly suggest you save it for after the briefing."

"I'll do that, ma'am."

Nova cleared her throat. "I'd like to reverse the usual order of things by asking Colonel Wolff if he has any questions for us, now that he's had an opportunity to familiarize himself with our strengths and weaknesses—strategically speaking, of course."

Wolff glanced around the table, trading covert smiles with Dana before beginning. "To put it bluntly, I think we're in for a world of trouble. Assuming that the figures I've been shown are accurate, we don't have sufficient mecha to engage the Invid, let alone mount a meaningful counteroffensive should their first wave be repulsed. Our stores of Protoculture are minimal and dangerously dispersed. And while some modicum of

firepower is concentrated at ALUCE, warships are out-
numbered ten to one by Veritech transports, which are
worthless in a fight. So, my question to you is simply
this: What stance do you plan to adopt when the Invid
arrive?"

The oversight committee chairman, Senator Pauli,
took up the challenge. "Having learned something from
Anatole Leonard, our initial position will be to adopt a
policy of watchful waiting. With the Masters, we
grasped, in due course, that they were coming for the
Protoculture Matrix, but we didn't even realize that we
had the damned thing until it was too late to sue for
peace. But from what you and Major Carpenter, among
others, have told us, the Invid are after these Flowers of
Life that have been sprouting like weeds all over the
world. So, it seems to me, straight off, that we have a
bargaining chip at our disposal."

"A bargaining chip," Wolff said, as if trying to com-
prehend Pauli's meaning.

"Yes. In the interest of framing a peaceful accord,
we'll allow the Invid free access to the Flowers, in return for their promise to respect our sovereignty over
the planet itself. Some show of force may be necessary
to convince them that we mean business, but that
shouldn't be too difficult to stage, from ALUCE or
some location downside."

Wolff was very aware of Dana Sterling's gaze. "Senator, excuse my saying so, but you're way off the mark.
The Invid are nothing like the Zentraedi or the Masters.
Get those notions out of your head. We're talking about
a race whose homeworld was defoliated, and who have
wreaked havoc on every world where their Flowers
took root and were detected. They don't announce their

arrival, and they don't engage in negotiations or accords. They sweep in and lay waste to everything and anything that hints at resistance. Then, very unceremoniously, they establish *themselves* as the sovereign power."

"Yes, Colonel, Major Carpenter has said as much," Alan Fredericks remarked in a patronizing tone. "But it seems to me that this scenario contradicts what you told us about the summit that took place aboard the SDF-3. Simulagent or not, that summit was doubtless an attempt at negotiation."

"But we were dealing with the *Regent*," Wolff argued. "And from everything the Sentinels learned, he's a different order of being than his spouse or feminine counterpart or whatever she is."

"This so-called Regis," Nova supplied.

Wolff nodded. "For all his savagery, the Regent has—or *had*—a Human streak. He patterned himself on the Masters. He's acquisitive and manipulative. He dreams of having what they had: an empire. That's why he could be drawn into negotiations."

"And this Regis?" one of the senators asked.

"She's searching for a homeworld."

"Then she'll have to look elsewhere," Pauli warned. "In the event she attacks first, we'll hit back with everything at our command. No holding back, as we did with the Masters. Retaliatory strikes by our squadrons of Logans and Veritechs will keep them outside lunar orbit. Why, you yourself said, Colonel, that they were defeated on every world in Tirol's local group."

"They were. But not by launching suicidal strikes."

"I caution the colonel to remember his place," Nova interjected.

Dana threw her a pointed glance. "With all due respect, ladies and gentlemen, Colonel Wolff and Major Carpenter are the only people in this room who have actually fought the Invid. They should at least be allowed to speak, without fear of censure."

"All right, Wolff," Pauli said a long moment later. "Suppose you tell us what you would do."

Wolff asked Nova to call up the data that had been downloaded from *The Homeward Bound* to the GMP's computers and to make it available to the keyboards and screens that were set into the table at every seat. Wolff typed in a flurry of commands, summoning high-resolution opticals of the huge, dimpled hemispheres that were the Invid's "dome hives."

"To begin with," he said, "we don't show the Regis our hand. We permit her to come and set up shop—in hives like the ones on-screen. She and her brood aren't bloodthirsty killers by nature. Like ants or vespids, they attack when provoked."

Wolff placed his hands flat on the table. "That's not to say that there won't be heavy casualties during the first couple of weeks of their occupation, regardless of our response. After her encounters with the Zentraedi and the Masters' Bioroids, she's going to figure that she has to pound us into submission. But we can minimize our losses by evacuating the cities—particularly those within a thousand miles of Monument—by withholding fire, and by insisting that everyone remain in the shelters until we've issued an all clear. They'll fashion their farms and hives where they find the choicest Flowers. And it's likely that anyone who puts up a resistance is going to end up a worker on one of those farms. But that's inevitable, in any case."

Pauli was aghast. "Are you seriously proposing that we sit by and allow ourselves to be turned into *slaves*?"

"Only for a time, Senator," Wolff answered calmly. "Once the Invid have full access to the Flowers and the nutrient they derive from them, some of the anger and fight will go out of them, and we can begin to make our move."

"We counterattack," Fredericks said.

But Wolff shook his head. "We fight them guerrilla style, hive to hive, from a series of small bases, until we've so disrupted their communication network that an attack on the main hive is warranted."

He called up opticals and schematics of Invid Scout ships, Armored Scouts, Troopers, and Shock Troopers—hulking, bipedal, insectile things, ten to twenty feet high, with Cyclopean eyespots and pincerlike arms. "They're easy to kill once you get the hang of it. Drones, basically, with little initiative, typically fighting in small groups."

"And just where do you propose we hide our mecha while they are 'setting up shop?' " Fredericks asked nastily.

"We keep most of our Alphas on the moon, which the Invid will ignore because it can't support the Flowers. Then, when the Regis has built her central hive, we begin to move mecha down the well to predetermined locations from which the hive can be attacked, but aren't close enough to present an overt threat."

"And these fortified locations would be ignored?" Pauli said in disbelief.

"Deals can be cut with the hive Enforcers. Each hive—whether a dome or a stilt—is responsible for delivering a quota of Flower nectar to the central hive. By helping the small hives meet those quotas, we'll be able to fortify our bases without too much interruption."

"By providing the hives with slaves, you mean," Nova said.

Wolff rocked his head. "I choose to call them volunteer field operatives."

Pauli snorted in derision. "Colonel Wolff, you could probably sell your idea of 'volunteer field operatives' in Tokyo, judging by what Lieutenant Sterling has told us of the climate there. Perhaps in some areas of the Southlands, as well. But I suspect we will be hard-pressed to convince the UEG, Defense Force command, and the people who support us to embrace such a ... such a humiliating plan." He studied Wolff for a moment. "Do you have anything further to add before we move on?"

Wolff made his lips a thin line. *Fools*, he thought. Earth's only hope rested with the REF. *The Homeward Bound* would have to fold for Tirol as soon as possible. "How long before we attack the Sensor Nebula?" he asked.

Pauli glanced at Nova. "I believe that Miss Satori has something to say on that matter."

"Colonel, we want to take a close look at your ship before sending it against the Nebula," Nova began. She gestured to the goggle-wearing civilian. "Mr. Nichols, along with a group of researchers who have been working in Tokyo, have proposed that the drives of *The Homeward Bound* can be made foldworthy."

Despite his best efforts, Wolff shot to his feet. "You're going to allow a bunch of techs to tamper with the only warship we have?"

"Who said anything about tampering?" Louie asked.

"We just want to have a look at the drives to see if anything can be done to reconfigure them."

Wolff started to reply, but faltered. Would Nichols be able to determine that the ship was, in fact, foldworthy? With Lang and Penn on Tirol, and Lazlo Zand and his people dead, was there anyone on Earth who possessed that depth of knowledge?

"The oversight committee has selected Lieutenant Sterling to head up the survey team," Fredericks said. "Naturally, Colonel, we expect you to accompany and familiarize them with the workings of the ship."

"But what about the Nebula mission?" Wolff managed to ask.

Fredericks smiled without showing his teeth. "First things first, Colonel."

CHAPTER ELEVEN

> ALUCE had its share of deserters following Leonard's decision to turn the facility into a Southern Cross base. Many of the decamping scientists, engineers, and technicians ended up in the Southlands, bringing with them not only their expertise but in many cases apparatus and supplies, including shuttles and construction robots liberated from ALUCE before the military arrived. And much of the state-of-the-art equipment would find its way to the Starchildren, who put it to immediate use.
>
> Weverka T'su,
> *Aftermath: Geopolitical and Religious Movements in the Southlands*

IN CENTRAL ARGENTINA, SOUTHWEST OF BUENOS Aires, under the retractable wings of a massive dome that had somehow escaped the Masters' notice despite its outward similarity to an Invid hive, sat an almost-completed, lozenge-shaped ship its builders hoped would one day take them to the stars. Assembled over the course of ten years by cadres of engineers, designers, and specialists of every discipline—some of whom had participated in the reconstruction and retrofitting of the SDF-1 on Macross Island—the ship had been christened *Napperson's Hope*, after the woman who had originally conceived the project.

A Robotech systems analyst who had studied under Emil Lang, Kaaren Napperson had become convinced—long before the Zentraedi attack of 2009—that Earth was destined to find itself embroiled in a lengthy and ultimately Human-fatal war, brought about by the controlled-crash arrival of the Visitor—the SDF-1. Caught up in the SDF-1's inadvertent jump to Pluto, however, Napperson had spent two years on board the ship she had helped restore; the following three working on the ill-fated SDF-2; and the next four in the null-gee center of the factory satellite, overseeing the transformation of Breetai's flagship into the SDF-3. It was only in 2019 that she had literally come down to Earth and relocated to the Southlands; and it was there she had gathered the personnel who would begin work on the ship of her dreams—a ship without weapons of any sort, whose purpose was to house and preserve at least a few specimens of the Human species before time ran out.

The so-called Starchildren had not begun as a cult; the news media were to blame for the name, which found common acceptance after Napperson's perhaps inevitable affiliation with the Church of Interstellar Retribution. Regardless, as word of the project spread, more and more people wanted to lend a hand in its realization, until there were more people living and working in the vicinity of the dome than the ship within could ever accommodate. And even when this became apparent, people weren't dissuaded from coming. Thanks to the lottery Napperson had devised, everyone stood an equal chance of making the final cut of twenty-five hundred passengers. Many believed, as well, that if one ship could be successfully launched, then that ship could be duplicated, and that eventually there would be space for any and all who wished to quit the planet before war reduced it to a barren, hopelessly irradiated ruin.

The Starchildren's motto—"Space for any and all"—referred as much to the lottery as to the fact that the cultists had no real destination other than the void between the stars. Napperson and her teams had utmost faith in the antigravity generators they had fashioned to levitate the ship; but lacking spacefold generators or Reflex furnaces, the ship couldn't even get *nowhere* fast.

Destination was beside the point, in any case. For the Starchildren viewed *Napperson's Hope* as an ark that would wander the galaxy for generations, breeding a new kind of Human. A new kind of *Earth* Human, that is, given the many diverse species known to inhabit the planets of distant star systems.

In itself, the galaxy's sheer abundance of intelligent life was enough to convince Napperson's followers that they would chance upon a species, which, like themselves, viewed war as an abomination . . .

Minutes into the VIP tour that had been arranged for her and Terry, Misa experienced a sense of nostalgia for a place she was visiting for the first time. She could almost believe that she had been there before—in a past life or something. She was not only astounded by what the Starchildren had created, but profoundly moved by their selfless commitment. More so than the residents of Tokyo, the Starchildren seemed to embody the indomitable spirit of the Human race. And they hadn't had to burrow underground to express it.

Just then, she and Terry were meeting with Kaaren Napperson herself, along with her husband and several others, in a cluttered office that overlooked the ship and the bustle that surrounded it. The dogged activity brought to mind the early days of the geo-grid, when Tokyo seemed to be excavating the future.

"You'll excuse me for saying so, Terry," Kaaren Napperson was remarking, "but your visit comes as quite a surprise." She was a handsome woman of sixty or so, with shoulder-length gray hair and big, blue-gray eyes.

"Mr. Shimada knew it would," Terry told her, a container of coffee in hand. "And we're encouraged that you could set aside your wariness, at least for the time being."

Napperson traded looks with her much-younger husband, Eric Baudel, a slight, balding man with hairy, muscular forearms. "To be honest, Terry, I'm not sure we have set aside our wariness."

Eiten Shimada had paved the way for Terry and Misa's visit. That had been accomplished easily enough, since the Nappersons had been trying to solicit Shimada interest in their project for the past several years. Also, Kaaren knew Terry from the time she had spent in Monument City in '24, when she had been asked to investigate a glitch that was plaguing the Alpha Veritech. That glitch had ultimately been traced to cyber-control experiments being conducted by one of Anatole Leonard's minions, the brilliant though misguided Joseph Petrie.

"Are we to assume that the Shimada Family has finally taken an interest in what we're trying to accomplish here?" Eric Baudel asked.

"The Shimadas have always taken an interest."

"Now they're considering taking a more active interest," Misa added.

Terry seemed pleased with the confusion their statements sowed. " 'Why now?' you're probably asking yourselves. Why, after all these years? Well, it all has to do with the ship that recently arrived from Tirol."

"Colonel Wolff's ship," Kaaren said. "But what does that have to do with us, or the Shimadas?"

"Before I tell you," Terry said, "you have to understand that the Shimadas think of Tokyo in much the same way you do your ship. As a kind of ark."

"We've said as much," Baudel thought to point out. "But where Tokyo's future is largely dependent on the very ground in which it's ensconced, *Napperson's Hope* will be a world unto itself."

Terry put his tongue in his cheek and nodded. "Assuming you can launch it before the Invid arrive."

"We're certainly working toward that end," Kaaren told him. "We could launch tomorrow—"

"But you have concerns about the ship's power core."

Kaaren smirked. "We've never tried to hide that fact, Terry. But given a choice, wouldn't you rather have the power of a sports car at your disposal than a Volkswagen? The fuel for sustained burns has always been our major problem."

"The Shimadas understand that. That's why we want to suggest that some of the parts you need have arrived—from Tirol."

Napperson, Baudel, and the others regarded one another in uncertain dismay. "That ship is REF property," Kaaren said at last. "And the Shimadas are very much mistaken if they think we'd stoop to piracy to realize our aims."

"These are desperate times for Humankind," Misa said on cue. "The Shimadas fear that the REF ship will be used to attack the Invid the moment they appear in Earthspace, and that it will be destroyed as a result."

"Your sports car, Kaaren," Terry interjected. "Reflex furnaces capable of propelling a ship to better than light speed. The Starchildren's ticket out of here."

Kaaren shook her head in disbelief. "Yes, and all we have to do is steal it out from under the noses of the GMP and the Tactical Armored Space Corps."

"That's where we come in," Terry said, without missing a beat. "What if I told you that we'll soon be in a position to provide you with information about the ship's security, Reflex drives, and other features. All you'd have to do is launch *Napperson's Hope* and position it where it can receive and make best use of the data."

"Terry . . ." Kaaren started to say, but he spoke over her.

"We're not saying that you have to do anything with what we provide you. But bear in mind that once you people leave Earthspace, you're essentially home free. There's not a ship between here and Tirol that could catch you."

"Of course, the Shimadas can't afford to take a direct hand in the matter," Misa quickly added. "But they can provide funding for what you'll need to launch *Napperson's Hope*."

"In exchange for what?" Baudel demanded to know. "Our promise to make room for them aboard?"

"Nothing of the sort," Terry said. "They're thinking only of the survival of our species."

Baudel made a plosive sound and sat back in his chair, shaking his head back and forth. "You seem to forget that only twenty-five hundred of us will be leaving. The people left behind will have to live with the stigma of our actions."

Terry mirrored Baudel's posture and spread his hands in a gesture of wily openness. "We're not twisting your arm, Eric. We're simply saying that we'd like to contribute to the success of your project."

Misa felt a shiver of longing pass through her. Gazing at the rapt expressions on the faces of Napperson and some of the others, she suddenly wanted nothing more than to see the Starchildren get their wish.

"Maybe Senator Pauli and the rest were taken in by Wolff's performance, but I'm not," General Vincinz told the dozen members of the now-defunct Southern Cross command. Two weeks had passed since the briefing at GMP headquarters, and the group was meeting in secret conclave in the back room of a strip club in Denver. "From what I hear, Wolff leaped out of his chair when Pauli informed him that a bunch of Tokyo geeks had been granted permission to survey his cherished ship."

"Can you blame the man?" Senator Grass said. "Who knows what damage they could do?"

Vincinz gestured dismissively. "Damage, my ass. Wolff's worried that they're going to discover the truth."

"Which truth is that?" the general's adjutant, Major Stamp, asked.

Vincinz leaned forward in his chair, resting his elbows on his knees and interlocking his blunt fingers. The room smelled of body odor and stale beer, and was faintly illuminated by colored ceiling spots. The stage and the chrome poles the strippers wrapped themselves around sat in darkness.

"Emil Lang wouldn't have dispatched a second ship on a one-way trip to Earth," Vincinz said. "I'll stake my life on it that that ship is foldworthy, and that Wolff is just itching to get his crew back on board so they can fold out of the mess they've landed in."

Everyone took a moment to consider the possibility. Senator Grass was the first to speak. "Are Shimada's people clever enough to determine the capacity of the fold generators?"

Vincinz nodded, narrow eyed. "Maybe even too clever. Think about it: All at once the Shimadas change their minds about giving us a look at their research—providing that their people are allowed a look at Wolff's ship. Why? Because ole Kan Shimada-*san* has his own suspicions about Wolff. I mean, what's to stop the Shimadas from cutting a deal with Wolff to be included among his cargo in exchange for keeping their mouths shut about the fold generators?"

Grass snorted a laugh. "Kan Shimada would never abandon Tokyo—even for a shot at immortality. It doesn't get much better than what he's already created for himself."

Vincinz conceded the point. "All right, maybe he wouldn't leave. But he might expect Wolff to pay for Tokyo's silence in other ways—in Protoculture or weapons."

Captain Bortuk, Vincinz's ferret-faced chief of staff, shook his head. "The last thing the Shimadas want are weapons. And as for Wolff smuggling 'culture down to Tokyo, I don't see how we can prevent it. Unless, of course, we're willing to share our suspicions with the GMP."

"We don't need to go that far," Vincinz said bitterly.

"The way I see, all we have to do is keep Wolff away from that ship."

"You're too late," Grass said. "He and that Tokyo bunch are already on their way."

"I'm talking about making sure that Wolff isn't assigned the Nebula mission."

Grass pulled down the corners of his mouth. "Unfortunately, we no longer have much say in that. Although, I suppose we could argue that Wolff and his crew—having fought the Invid on Tirol and elsewhere—are too vital to our defenses to place at risk."

Vincinz grinned wickedly. "That's the idea. We need Wolff and his people to advise us. Ideally, we would want to get some of our own people assigned to the Nebula mission."

"That mission isn't exactly going to be a cakewalk," Bortuk commented. "There's high probability that the Sensor Nebula isn't as innocuous as it appears to be. I've read Rolf Emerson's after-mission reports on the counterattack Leonard launched against the Masters' fleet. Some of the pilots under Emerson's command who passed closest to the cloud reported serious problems with their mecha. Spontaneous reconfiguration, scrambled communications, laser malfunctions . . . So why not let the GMP have run of the mission, rather than jeopardize any of our own people?"

"Because we would benefit from familiarizing ourselves with the ship." Vincinz paused for a moment. "Particularly in advance of our commandeering it."

"Are you out of your mind?" Grass's voice was shrill with disbelief. "What do we want with that ship?"

Vincinz grinned faintly. "Power. The power Aldershot, Constanza, and the rest are afraid to hurl against the Invid. The power to reassert the authority of the Southern Cross. The power to determine our own fate in the coming war. And one final thing: a way out of it."

"The war?" Major Stamp said dubiously.

Vincinz nodded. "Pretend for a moment that I'm right about Wolff and the ship. Or, if you don't like that, consider that Shimada's geeks will be able to work some magic on the fold generators."

Stamp ran a hand over his mouth. "All right, but how's that provide us with an 'out'? Where are we going to go—to Pluto?"

"Tirol," Vincinz replied evenly.

Grass stared at him, then burst out laughing. "That's rich, Vincinz. With Edwards probably hanging from his boot heels in Tiresia? I'm sure Reinhardt and Hunter would love to have a couple of more Southern Cross *renegades* drop in on them."

"To hell with Edwards," Vincinz snapped. "And how would Hunter know we weren't sent to Tirol by the UEG? They won't have a clue. Besides, we'd be doing the REF a service by apprising them of what's been happening on Earth." He glanced pointedly at everyone. "Where would you rather be: here, condemned to some Flower of Life labor camp, or there, cozying up to Mr. and Mrs. Hunter with a couple of elaborate lies of omission?"

"Seems a risk either way," Grass said, relenting somewhat. "After all, we don't know what's been happening on *Tirol*. We could be jumping from the frying pan to the fire."

Vincinz shrugged nonchalantly. "I'll take the fire over the long sizzle. I didn't enjoy waiting for the Masters, and I know I'm not going to enjoy waiting for the Invid. And the way Wolff makes it sound, we're going to get our asses kicked no matter what we do. So where's the harm in our leaving? My guess is that by the time we return to Earth, there won't be a person alive who could denounce us for what we did."

The Homeward Bound had neither the blockish, articular countenance of the SDF-1, nor the bulbous, organic mien of the SDF-3. In profile the modified Garfish approximated the fore-tapered sleekness of the deep-sea denizen after which it had been named, though it was cinched amidships by a beltlike housing, from which hung a fish-shaped spacefold module. Twice the length of the Garfish HSTC frigates the SDF-3 had carried in its belly to Tirol, the ship contained more than eighty mecha in its belly and had space for a crew of six hundred, though *The Homeward Bound* had arrived with a force only half that size.

Wolff had supplied opticals and schematics of some of the other prototypes the REF had manufactured in Tirolspace, including considerably modified versions of the bird-of-prey Horizont DTTS and the goliath Ikazuchi Command Carrier. But of all of them, the Garfish alone looked as though it would have been at home among the dreadnoughts of the Zentraedi Grand Fleet.

The shuttle that had lofted Dana, Wolff, Louie, and the Tokyo tech detachment docked alongside the Garfish, and everyone cycled through the air locks without incident—though Gibley and company remained nauseated until well after they were safely on board. As an accommodation to them, *The Homeward Bound*'s artificial gravity had been enabled by the GMP and TASC guards who had been stationed aboard the ship since Wolff and crew had debarked for ALUCE a month earlier.

Once over their queasiness, Gibley, Shi Ling, Strucker, and the others began to behave like kids on a school trip to a hands-on museum. The only old hand among them—having flown combat missions upside and toured the interiors of many a warship—Louie was slightly more reserved, though Dana could see that even he was itching to disassemble some component to see how it functioned. Wolff had further supplied that the ship's spacefold generators were not empowered by Karbarran Flower of Life peat, as Carpenter's had been, but by a more conventional dialogue between unadulterated Protoculture and the monopole ore the REF Zentraedi had mined on Fantoma. But while it seemed unlikely that the generators could be revitalized by Earth technology, no one appeared discouraged. Except for Wolff, of course, who was beside himself with concern. So, in a sincere effort to distract him, Dana suggested that he show her around the bridge while Shimada's team went to work.

Compared to the SDF-3, or indeed to the now-crippled destroyers of the Southern Cross fleet, *The Homeward Bound* felt cramped and disorderly. The passageways were narrow and in many cases unlighted, and only a few of the cabin spaces were finished. Conduits and fiber-optic lines were exposed, and most of the partitions had obviously been erected in haste. The bridge was a variation on the tried-and-true design incorporated into the SDFs, though almost intimate in its proportions. Centered among the various duty stations sat the signature, solitary command chair, with its vantage of the two forward viewports. And taking up most of the starboard bulkhead was the vertical stack of monitors that comprised the threat-assessment display.

Dana seated herself at one of the forward stations. The lunar surface seemed near enough to touch, and she calculated that the large bright spot at one o'clock was the factory satellite, where repairs to the iris gate had commenced. Wolff took the adjacent chair and stared at the moon for a long moment before speaking.

"My first day on the factory satellite, I remember thinking that there couldn't possibly be a planet as beautiful as Earth. And now when I look out there, I find myself comparing Earth to worlds like Karbarra and Garuda and what was Praxis. Even Haydon IV and Tirol have their fine points—though Tirol's only a moon, and a rather forlorn one at that."

"It's so incredible that you've seen those places," Dana said.

He turned to her and smiled. "Maybe you'll see them one day, after all this is over and done with. Your father was always saying how he wished you could see this or that place. You were never out of his thoughts, you know."

His words brought a lump to her throat. "I wish I could remember Max more clearly. Miriya, too. But I just have these vague memories. And I can't even sort out the real ones from all the stories Rolf told me."

"If your folks had had even a hint of what was to come, they never would have left Earth. They would have resigned their commissions."

"But then I might not have a younger sister."

"Or maybe you'd have more than one."

She laughed at that, and listened intently while Wolff

began to elaborate on some of the incidents he had touched on during the shuttle flight from ALUCE. He talked about Max's exploits with the Sentinels and about Miriya's close friendship with the members of the Praxian Sisterhood, and how she had saved the life of a Spherisian named Teal. He spoke, too, of his belief that Miriya's pregnancy had been influenced by the exotic atmosphere of Garuda, and by something called the *hin*.

Dana loved listening to him, and she couldn't wait to repeat for Bowie what Wolff had to say about Bowie's parents, Jean and Vince. She mapped Wolff's face with her eyes, and she catalogued his seemingly unlimited repertoire of expressions, which shifted continuously and seemed to draw her in all the more.

At some point he went from talking about the Grants to talking about his wife and son, whom he had apparently met with in Denver, though things hadn't gone well. And almost confessionally he revealed that he had been unfaithful to Catherine on Tirol. He had fallen in love with Lynn-Minmei, of all people, only to crash and burn when she had taken up with T. R. Edwards. More than taken up with: had *married* in a bizarre ceremony aboard Edwards' ship, during its desperate flight to Optera.

"I came this close to killing Edwards with my bare hands," Wolff said, regarding his fists, "just after the trial. Like all cowards, he ran, and I chased him, convinced that I was going to kill him if I caught him. But I collided with a young kid—Lang's nephew, I think it was, Scott something-or-other—and Edwards got away. I'm sure that he kidnapped Minmei. I know she wouldn't have gone with him of her own free will."

Dana wrestled with the irritation his statements

roused. Why was he taking responsibility for Minmei's actions? What compelled everyone to feel so over-protective toward her? Just because she was The Voice that had helped defeat the Zentraedi? The problem was that most people simply didn't know her as Dana did—that is, as well as Max and Miriya and Lisa Hayes knew her. They didn't know what a self-serving little priss she could be, and how she had jerked Rick Hunter around for years. Why, she wouldn't even be on Tirol if she hadn't arranged to be caught up in the SDF-3's spacefold—and she'd only done that to remain close to Rick, surely in the hope that he and Lisa would fall on hard times. And while she was waiting for that to happen, she had snared Jonathan in her web—

"You shouldn't condemn yourself for being attracted to Minmei," Dana said suddenly. "You were far from home, and she's a seductive . . . woman."

"That she is," Wolff mused. "But I can't help wondering, if she hadn't gotten involved with Edwards . . ."

"Would you still have made the decision to return to Earth?"

He nodded. "How do I know I'm not just running back to Catherine on the rebound?"

His right hand was on the console between them, and Dana reached for it without thinking. "That's why you're here—to find out."

Wolff held her gaze for a long moment, then blew out his breath and swiveled his chair to face the bulkhead hatch. "We'd better go check on your friend, Louie, and the rest of them. I don't want them thinking they have run of this ship."

No sooner had he said it and stood up than Louie

came through the hatch, with his goggles pushed up onto his high forehead and a defeated look on his face.

"Is there any hope?" Dana asked, hurrying to him.

Louie shrugged. "Gibley's never seen anything like it. The power-core module is effectively designed to clip onto the ship, which suggests that Lang's design teams mean for the driver to be interchangeable. But it's alien technology. It'll be months before we analyze even a fraction of the data stored in the ship's computers."

"And the spacefold generators?"

Louie slipped the goggles down over his eyes. "Good for a one-way trip."

Dana and Wolff sighed at the same time. Though, later, it would occur to her that his sigh seemed informed more by relief than disappointment.

CHAPTER TWELVE

Much as the Internal Revenue Service had not only survived but prospered during the Global Civil War and the First Robotech War, the GMP emerged from the Masters' War [sic] as a more powerful entity than it had ever been. This reversal of fortune, however, was less a consequence of the deaths of Leonard and Moran than the deaths of sixty-four Southern Cross–friendly delegates, who had been killed in the Masters' strike on the Senate Building in Monument City. As it happened, the building had two underground shelters, one of which was favored by members of the Southern Cross old-boy network, and the other by those politicos who had risen to power with the Robotech Defense Force; and the Masters' light fell on the Southern Cross side ... Not three months after the end of the Masters' War, the GMP enjoyed what amounted to absolute authority to detain, arrest, search and seize, surveil, infiltrate, and subvert as the agency saw fit. And in this, the GMP couldn't have been served better than by deputy directors Colonel Alan Fredericks and Lieutenant Nova Satori.

"Upheaval," *History of the Third Robotech War,* Volume III

THE SHIMADAS HAD ARRANGED A HERO'S WELCOME for Gibley's team—including Louie Nichols—just arrived from three days of intense debriefing at GMP headquarters. Held at Kan Shimada's palatial home in the geo-grid, the celebration featured singers and costumed dancers, bubble-blowing machines, storms of flower petals, and cases of *ramune*—old-fashioned ginger ale, served in bottles sealed with glass marbles. Attendance was mandatory for all upper-echelon members of the Family, a group that totaled some two hundred people. Terry Weston had returned from the Southlands just to attend; though Misa, captivated by the Starchildren's flourishing base of operations, had opted to remain in Argentina a while longer.

It was not, however, until the inner circle had retired to the estate's Edo-style garden teahouse that Kan Shimada broached the subject of *The Homeward Bound*, and then only after tea had been ceremoniously served and a measure of dusk had been imparted to the artificial sky. What with the diffuse sunset effects and the cherry trees lining the moat, you could almost believe you were on the surface.

"As all of you are aware," Kan Shimada told his sons and advisers, "I have never—much to my regret—ventured higher than one hundred thousand feet above our world. I have fond memories of the years before the Rain, when we talked of building a resort on the moon, and of raising pyramid and volcano-shaped cities on Earth. I regret, too, that the imminent arrival of the Masters compelled us to withdraw our financial support from Mars Base—though in light of what occurred we were certainly judicious to do so.

"Outer space has long fascinated me, but destiny has drawn me inward, as it were. And yet"—he glanced at Gibley's team, who occupied places of honor at the table—"with our having been allowed to survey the interior of Colonel Wolff's ship, I now feel that I have journeyed—in proxy—at least partway to the stars."

Shimada fell silent for a moment. "Let us go to the heart of the matter," he then said. "Can the ship be induced to fold?" He directed the question to Gibley; but—with a look—Gibley handed it off to Louie.

"*The Homeward Bound* is already fold capable," Louie announced to surprised murmurs from everyone but Kan Shimada. "Thanks to Gibley's way with intelligent machines, we were able to wring enough out of the on-board computer to learn that Protoculture levels are much higher than anyone would be led to believe. Lang's technicians fashioned some clever camouflage, but Protoculture has a way of revealing itself. That's how the Masters were able to zero in on the burial site of the SDF-1. They scanned for the Protoculture Matrix."

Kan Shimada's expression was unreadable. "Is Colonel Wolff merely being, shall we say, discreet, or is he himself in the dark as to the ship's capacities?"

"He definitely knows what he has," Gibley answered, "since he's the only key that can unlock the fold generators."

Unable to contain his enthusiasm, Louie spoke up. "The spacefold system is keyed to a voice-recognition code Wolff alone can supply. Without that code, we can't even converse with the generators, much less enable the system itself."

Shimada pressed the tips of his fingers together. "Given time, could we supply the machine with a facsimile of the code?"

"We're already working on that, Mr. Shimada," Gibley said. "But we'd stand a better chance if we could revisit the ship."

Shimada nodded in understanding. "Then, in order to ensure our remaining on good terms with them, we must begin to provide the GMP and the Defense Force with something of value. The Southern Cross never took much interest in artificial intelligence and robotics, but perhaps if we showed them some of our results . . ."

Gibley was nodding his head. "One thing we could

do is try to interest them in sending a robot-crewed ship against the Invid Sensor Nebula."

"Pursue that course," Shimada encouraged. "And in the meantime, continue to work on deciphering Wolff's code." He cut his eyes to Louie. "Is it your assumption that the fold generators have been pretasked to return the ship to Tirol?"

"I'm leaning in that direction. Lang seems to have relied heavily on the technology that the Masters incorporated into the Zentraedi ships. *The Homeward Bound* is designed to be user friendly by personnel with limited expertise, and, in effect, is capable of executing a wide range of programs on its own. Wolff doesn't have to submit to a retinal scan or a vein scan to enable the spacefold generators. All he has to do is give the code. And that's certainly deliberate on Lang's part, because he wanted the ship to remain operational even if something happened to Wolff. In fact, I'm willing to bet that the ship could execute a spacefold without *any* crew."

Shimada paused to consider the implications. "The ship could be sent away on its own?"

Louie nodded. "Properly prompted."

Shimada looked at Terry Weston. "It seems that we may have been premature in sending you and Misa to Argentina."

Terry's mouth twitched uncertainly. "We don't need their help, that's for sure. But maybe *we* can help *them*."

Shimada raised an eyebrow.

Terry said, "Louie, can more than one ship be folded during a jump?"

It was obvious that the question piqued Louie's curiosity, but he kept his thoughts to himself. "There's some precedent for it. Macross Island was folded to Plutospace along with the SDF-1. And it appears that a small ship carrying Lynn-Minmei and Janis Em was folded to Fantoma along with the SDF-3. But I'm not sure I'd want to risk hitching a ride that way."

Shimada glanced at Terry. "Your concern for them is commendable, Terry, but Louie is correct: folding in tandem is too unreliable, and too dangerous. In attempting to help them, we could end up thwarting them. Therefore, we must undo our mistake immediately. Inform our agent in Argentina to apprise her supposed handlers of the launch plans. But make certain our name doesn't come up."

"Hai," Terry said softly, inclining his head.

Shimada was quiet for a moment, then he looked at Gibley. "Without the code, we can do nothing?"

"Without the code, and Wolff to vocalize it," Gibley amended.

"Then we must first determine if Wolff can be enticed or coerced into revealing the code. I want to hear your thoughts on the matter."

Gibley locked his hands behind his head and smirked. "Well, he and Dana Sterling seemed to be getting pretty chummy."

Slowly, everyone turned to Louie, who was still trying to make sense of Kan and Weston's veiled conversation about Argentina. "Would Dana Sterling be likely to assist in our efforts, or to undermine them?" Shimada asked.

Louie pondered the questioned, then smirked. "I think she'd be willing to help us. She has her own reasons for wanting to see that ship return to Tirol. A hundred and thirty of them, to be exact."

* * *

"The Starchildren are planning to *raid* Wolff's ship?" Alan Fredericks said to Nova in a tone of amused incredulity. "And just how are they planning to do that, with *The Homeward Bound* two hundred thousand miles away?"

"Our informant wasn't specific on that point. But apparently they're planning to use their own ship to get them there."

The skepticism in Fredericks's bemused smile deepened. "Weren't we given to understand—by this same informant—that *Napperson's Hope* was just that: more pipe dream than promise?"

"They've found some new financial backers."

"Who?"

Nova shook her head. "Our girl didn't say."

"Couldn't say or wouldn't?"

"She'll tell everything she knows for a single-payment bonus of three million dollars."

Fredericks made a *tsk*ing sound. "Greedy little thing, isn't she?"

They were in Fredericks's office in GMP headquarters, where serious renovation work was in progress. The whine of power tools infiltrated the room, which smelled strongly of joint compound and acrylic primer. Fredericks's desk was an oak antique, piled high with computer tapes and hard-copy reports. The fixed-pane window overlooked the parking lot and the foothills of the Rockies. Only two years earlier, the cubical building had been a hotel.

Fredericks drummed his fingers on the desktop, while Nova took a moment to inspect the active-length nails of her right hand. "Have you discussed this offer with Aldershot?" he asked after a moment.

"He wants us to handle it."

"Of course. Now that he's been bumped up to commander of Tactical Space Corps, he has no time for the mundane world of intelligence gathering."

Nova shrugged. "Something like that. He isn't convinced about the Starchildren information, but he did suggest that we respond as if."

"Lest the GMP be caught with its pants down." Fredericks sniffed. "Well, I refuse to be pumped for additional funds. Not another dollar goes to our informant. The identity of Napperson's backers, in any account, isn't crucial to our response. Do you think Napperson realizes that Wolff's ship is incapable of executing a spacefold?"

That information had been supplied by Louie Nichols and the Shimada team on their return from *The Homeward Bound*. Debriefed, they had been released a week earlier. It remained to be seen just what research data Shimada would turn over to the Defense Force, now that the GMP had lived up to its side of the bargain.

"Napperson's obviously willing to settle for Reflex furnaces, in a pinch," Nova said. "What's more, she probably feels that she'll be doing Earth a favor by further reducing our arsenal."

Fredericks shook his head in transparent disapproval. "Sounds as though she and old man Shimada would make the perfect couple. Perhaps the Invid Regis will award them merit badges for their efforts in her behalf." He sighed. "Well, I don't see that we have any choice but to delay their launch schedule."

Nova brushed her hair away from her face. "Seems a shame, after all they've accomplished."

"They'll have themselves to blame. I'm disappointed, though, that the Starchildren would resort to sedition. Not to mention that they would fail to consider that we'd get wind of their plans. Still, as much as I dislike our informant, I think it's best to carry out our directive without compromising her. Who knows, she may decide to supply us with the name of Napperson's most recent convert free of charge."

Nova quirked a cunning smile. "Do you have a subcontractor in mind?"

Fredericks nodded. "A competitor, you might say."

"I didn't know that the Starchildren had any competitors."

"For Wolff's ship, they do." Fredericks waited for Nova's surprise to show, then added, "We need simply to arrange for General Vincinz to hear of Napperson's plans. Given the Southern Cross interest in Wolff's ship, I suspect that everything will see to itself from that point on."

Nova nodded in comprehension. "Speaking of Wolff, there's growing concern about his taking part in the Nebula mission."

Fredericks's brow furrowed. "What's behind that, do you suppose?"

"I can only tell you what I've been hearing."

Fredericks's thin fingers made a beckoning gesture.

"Now that the ship's been off-loaded of data and REF mecha, people are saying that Wolff and his crew are too valuable to risk on an operation that's not only dangerous but of questionable worth to begin with."

"Do you concur?" Fredericks asked her.

She shrugged. "There's some wisdom in it."

"Who, then?"

Nova smiled without showing her teeth. Two could play Fredericks's game. "I have a candidate in mind."

Fredericks leaned forward to watch her prize a thick intel report from her briefcase. The report's red cover told him that it had come from the lab of the late Lazlo Zand.

Skids stacked high with cargo crates crowded the greasy floor of the GMP armory building in Denver. All of it had been shuttled down the well from *The Home-ward Bound*, which remained in lunar orbit. Wooden bleachers had been erected along the walls of the spacious, high-ceilinged room, and nearly every inch of bench seat was occupied by GMP, TASC, and Southern Cross personnel.

Jonathan Wolff, wearing a tight-fitting REF uniform, moved commandingly among the crates and a dozen REF officers, including Major John Carpenter. A wireless microphone clipped to the collar of Wolff's tunic carried his tenor voice throughout the room, and a trio of huge, overhead display screens supplied real-time close-ups of weapons and mecha, or battle footage of Invid assault craft and Inorganics.

"It's possible that we won't be going up against the Hellcats, the Jack Knives, and the Blue Eyes," Wolff was saying, referring to the ghoulish, long-armed robots that were marching across the display screens. "The Regent employed them primarily as occupation forces, and rarely as frontline troops. But there's no evidence to suggest that the *Regis* will employ them. That's why we'll be stressing tactics more appropriate for combat against the Scout, Trooper, and Shock Trooper assault units, all of which are outfitted with a type of chitinous armor, and are equipped with plasma-disk delivery systems."

Dana was sitting in the upper-tier bleachers, close to the armory's principal doorway. Having arrived late, she had missed Wolff's introductory remarks about the weapons of the REF arsenal, which, by Earth standards, were almost fifteen years out of date—or out of fashion, at any rate.

At the insistence of Anatole Leonard—who loathed anything that smacked of the Robotech Defense Force—the Army of the Southern Cross had mothballed much of what had been developed for the Expeditionary mission. Hovertanks, A-JACs, and Logans had taken precedence over the Alpha and Beta Veritechs, the Destroids, and the Alpha-portable Light Combat Cyclones. Hermes helmets and flare-shouldered torso harnesses had replaced CVR-3 Body Armor. And the Southern Cross had generated its own line of weapons to substitute for the R Burke–designed Gallant H-90, FAL-2 pulse laser rifle, SAL-9 single shot laser pistol, and Wolverine assault rifle.

However, the remnants of Leonard's army, deprived of much of their mecha, grasped that they were going to have to refamiliarize themselves with the arms and armaments of their former rivals if they expected to integrate with returning waves of REF forces—should they arrive from Tirol.

On returning from Wolff's ship, Dana had gone directly to the Emerson cabin. Fifteen more Tiroleans had died during her absence, and conditions at the compound had continued to deteriorate. Where she thought

Bowie would take heart from what Wolff had told her, the five-year-old stories about his parents, Jean and Vince, had only plunged Bowie deeper into desperation. She blamed herself for not having been able to predict as much from her own delayed reaction to Wolff's well-meaning words about Max and Miriya. And as for Sean and Angelo, they were about ready to re-up if something wasn't done about the Tiroleans.

There was no justification for her returning to Denver, or, indeed, for attending Wolff's discourse on battle tactics. After all, she was a diplomat now; even those she had fought alongside during the War had begun to treat her with a deference she wasn't accustomed to and didn't appreciate. But it didn't take much self-examination to realize that she had been missing Wolff—Jonathan. She wanted to convince herself that he was important to her as the sole link to her parents; but she knew it went deeper than that. She was enchanted with him, and not simply because his photo had graced the wall of her locker.

This wasn't a crush, it wasn't infatuation, and she refused to so much as consider the older-man-as-replacement-dad psychobabble she had heard from Rolf during her short-lived romance with Terry Weston. No, what she felt for Jonathan had welled up from her heart, and she couldn't dismiss it or explain it away, despite her best efforts. And tried she had, by reminding herself that Jonathan was not only fresh from a disastrous—though admittedly incomprehensible—affair with Lynn-Minmei, but that he had a wife and son with whom he was attempting to reconcile. Besides, who was she to think that he would have similar feelings for her, or that she had the right to step in and make matters worse for him?

Still, he had seen her enter the armory and he had made meaningful eye contact with her several times since . . .

Wolff's lecture lasted another three hours, only to conclude in heated debates between TASC and REF officers. What did a former Hovertank commander know about combat flying? the Cosmic Unit commanders argued. Just because he had ridden a star ship home from Tirol, Wolff was suddenly entitled to preferential treatment?

Also, many of the officers in the room resented Wolff for the parade the provisional government had staged. Weren't they owed one for having defeated the Masters? At the end, Wolff was practically shouting to be heard above an audience of disgruntled veterans, many of whom were filing through the exits in patent distrust.

"This is hopeless," Wolff was telling Carpenter and a couple of members of the Wolff Pack by the time Dana had worked her way down to him. "They have no faith in guerrilla tactics. They're used to meeting the enemy head-on, and they're convinced that the same approach is going to work against the Invid."

Everyone who had remained agreed and commiserated. The way Dana saw it, their devotion alone spoke to Wolff's abilities as a leader. Seeing her coming, however, they started to disperse, intent on providing Wolff with some private space.

He managed a sardonic smile for Dana. "What the hell's the good of being portrayed a hero if no one's willing to listen to you?"

"You have to be patient, Colonel," Dana said in a

low voice. "For better or worse, we were raised on a certain combat style, and the notion of hide-and-strike fighting is going to take some getting used to. But I do understand your frustration."

He gave her hand an affectionate squeeze. "Call me Jonathan, Dana."

She perched herself on the edge of one of the cargo crates and began to tell him of her own ambivalence about going back to war, and about the Tiroleans the 15th were sheltering from everything but dislocation and death, and about her yearning to be reunited with her parents.

"I know it sounds strange," she said. "I mean, I hardly remember Max and Miriya, but . . ."

"But what?" he encouraged, planting himself next to her.

She waited a long moment before saying, "Something happened to me on the Masters' flagship. I mistakenly grabbed hold of a canister of Protoculture and I experienced . . . well, a kind of hallucination. I know you'll think I'm crazy, but I saw my sister, Aurora, and Max and Miriya. They told me they were with the Sentinels, and they warned me that the Flowers of Life were going to draw the Invid to Earth." She looked at Wolff. "I saw them, Jonathan, almost as clearly as I'm seeing you now."

Nonplussed, Wolff stood up and paced away from her. "The Awareness," he said, turning to face her. "The artificial intelligence at the heart of Haydon IV. Somehow . . ." He shook his head.

Dana stared at him. "Jonathan, I don't understand."

He approached her and took hold of her hands. "All I'm trying to say is that your experience aboard the flagship wasn't just some hallucination. It was something *real*, Dana."

She wanted desperately to rid herself of the rest of the vision: that a ship would arrive to deliver her to Tirol. But she thought he might misinterpret her meaning, so she said nothing. What would be the point, anyway, when that ship obviously wasn't *The Homeward Bound*.

Unexpectedly, when she lifted her face to him, he kissed her softly on the mouth.

CHAPTER THIRTEEN

The identity of the operative the GMP infiltrated among the Starchildren had been the subject of much speculation and, at times, heated debate, until the matter was laid to rest by Shi Ling, in his posthumously published tome, Sometimes Even a Yakuza Needs a Place to Hide. *Her name was Martha Fox, and Shi Ling puts her age at fifty-five when she was killed in the Invid attack on the Starchildren's colony [January, 2033]. A first-rate mecha engineer, Fox was serving a twenty-year sentence in Monument's Bitteroot Correctional Facility for acts of [Zentraedi] terrorism committed during the Malcontent Uprising. Recruited by Nova Satori in 2031, Fox was sent to Argentina, where she rose effortlessly to a high-level position in the Starchildren cult, and became the mistress of [Kaaren Napperson's husband] Eric Baudel. Promised an even more lofty position in Tokyo, Fox was in turn recruited by Eiten Shimada, only to betray the Family the following year by selling information to the GMP about the Shimada's financial ties to the Starchildren.*

Channing DeMont, *The Secret History of the GMP*

MISA AND IZUMI SAUNTERED THROUGH Japantown, watching people going about their business. Shawls were being knitted, shoes mended, chickens plucked, bicycles repaired. Come sundown, the Argentine air could turn bitterly cold, but tonight there was no breeze sweeping in from the Andes and the temperature was almost balmy.

They held hands while they walked, as if it were the most natural thing in the world. Pairs of girls hurried past them, arm in arm; pairs of boys, as well, with their arms around each other's shoulders. The dirt streets were lighted by lanterns or solitary incandescent bulbs. A brew of appetizing aromas swirled in the air.

"I love it here," Misa told her new friend.

Izumi nodded in agreement. "That's why I couldn't care less about leaving."

"And when the ship launches?"

"We'll begin work on another one."

"And if the Invid come here?"

"We'll ask for their help."

Two weeks at the Starchildren's *pampas* colony—variously referred to as Launch City (Ciudad Lanzar), Napperson Naval Station, or Noah's Follow-up Folly—had confirmed Misa's first hunch about the place. The saucer ship was almost incidental. It was the dream itself that had drawn and continued to unite everyone. Half the people she'd met expressed little or no interest in leaving aboard *Napperson's Hope*; they were content merely to be part of the effort. And it was that pioneer spirit that distinguished the colony from Tokyo. For where the Starchildren were constructing a future—though for a relative few—Tokyo seemed intent on waiting one out.

In good-natured dismissal of Misa's protests, Kaaren Napperson and Eric Baudel had insisted on treating her as a VIP, which meant that she had been permitted to wander as she would, even into areas of the ship and its encompassing dome that were off-limits to all but the engineering elite of the Starchildren. Kan Shimada's ambassador of a sort, Misa had a motorized cart and driver at her beck and call, was free to question whomever she might, and dined nightly with Kaaren and Eric themselves, who sometimes seemed intent on adopting her.

The results of Tokyo's sudden generosity were already having a powerful impact on the colony—a trial launch was scheduled and final selection of the twenty-five hundred passengers was under way—so Misa could understand why the project chiefs would want to keep her happy and well fed. But their innocence troubled her. They had no notion of the favor they were doing the Shimadas by assisting in the disabling of Jonathan Wolff's ship.

From Tokyo, Terry had told her what he could about the initial survey of *The Homeward Bound*, which had apparently gone well—well enough, at any rate, for the Shimadas to have reciprocated by sharing technology with the Defense Force. Terry was being placed in charge of that; and Louie Nichols, the Shimada Building's newest fixture, was to serve as liaison with the GMP.

Given the number of deserters and "retirees" that had been turning up at the colony, it was a wonder to Misa that the Defense Force was still vital. Each day saw the arrival of soldiers and their families, from Monument, Mexico, Cavern, Brasília, Buenos Aires, and other cities strafed or ruined by the Masters. Misa listened to story after story detailing the horror of the attacks. And during each, she would find herself reflecting on how quiet Tokyo had been during the same period, the tranquility interrupted only by the occasional blare of the early-warning-system sirens, the economy bolstered through trade with other Asian and Pacific Rim centers.

The increase in immigration had led to tightened security throughout the colony, though primarily in the crowded residential zones that surrounded the dome. The interior of the dome was patrolled by a legion of fifteen-year-old Destroids, which were part of a larger arsenal of Veritechs, Logans, and Hovertanks. The Starchildren's militia, made up of some two thousand former soldiers, practiced regular drills, but had yet to be deployed against any threat, real or imagined. Argentina was far removed from what passed for the world's industrial centers, and those who came to the *pampas* usually had had their fill of war.

Without deliberately setting out to do so, Misa had found herself spending most of her time among the colony's sizable population of *Nihon-jin*. Many of them were the grandchildren and great-grandchildren of cattle ranchers and soybean farmers who had emigrated to the Amazon basin at the turn of the century, and the enclave they had fashioned for themselves was rich in traditions that had been abandoned by ethnically diverse, modern Tokyo. Ironically, the simple life Misa had sought since her youth in the communal orphanages was alive and well, there on the vast, rolling plains of the Southlands.

Izumi Sasaki had become her unofficial guide to the narrow streets that comprised Japantown. He was thin and always smiling, and only an inch shorter than her. They had met at a noodle shop and formed an instant friendship that gave every indication of harboring at least the seeds of romance. Izumi was in fact one of the main reasons she hadn't returned to Tokyo with Terry Weston.

Yes, she still loved Terry, but whatever future they might once have forged had been undermined by his reenlistment in the military—a military that had once branded him unfit for duty, no less. She had come to realize that she couldn't be partnered with a soldier; a soldier in the Defense Force, or for that matter, a soldier in the Shimada Family.

"So, do you love this place enough to delay your return to Tokyo?" Izumi asked her now. He knew that much about her—that she was visiting the Argentine—but not much else.

"I've already delayed my return by two weeks."

"And your family is missing you?"

She smiled inwardly. "Yes. I think so."

"You have a large family there?"

"Well, an extended one, anyway."

"Then you'll probably leave before the launch?"

"I might."

He sighed dramatically. "You're going to miss a great party."

She was about to reply when the ground shook with earthquake force and a deafening explosive report assaulted them from the northeast. Shaken, they turned in time to see an enormous fireball rise into the night sky.

Izumi's face was a mask of anguish. "The dome!" he said, in a tremulous voice. "The ship!"

Dana was aware that the Shimadas had sent Louie to Denver to negotiate with the GMP, but she hadn't expected him to arrive unannounced at the cabin. She had returned to Monument only two days earlier, largely in flight from Jonathan and the confusion brought on by the sudden and upsetting change in their relationship. Sean had shown Louie up the hill to where Dana and Angelo were utilizing one of the Hovertanks to excavate graves for the Tiroleans. Three more had succumbed since Dana's trip to Denver. At the same time, there was reason for cautious optimism, in that Bowie and Musica had succeeded in reprogramming one of Bowie's synthesizers to emulate the eerie harmonies and dissonances of the Cosmic Harp.

Louie's ever-present tinted goggles couldn't conceal his distress at seeing the grave sites, though it was equally apparent that his visit hadn't been prompted by concern for the health of the clones. Surely, his uneasiness had something to do with Shimada business. Even when he and Dana had put some distance between themselves and Sean and Angelo—much to their outrage—Louie remained agitated and wouldn't look her in the eye.

"Louie, will you quit pacing around and tell me what's on your mind!" she said at last. A cliff face along the ridge caught hold of her words and sent them echoing through the canyon.

He hemmed and hawed for a moment, then said, "Dana, it's *The Homeward Bound.* Wolff failed to mention that we wouldn't be able to penetrate the on-board computer because it's secured by a voice code. As it turns out, he's the only one with full access to the data."

Dana puzzled over the assertions. "Why would he conceal that from you?"

"We're not sure. Maybe the computer contains additional information about the Sentinels or the REF, or about the true purpose of his mission? We just don't know. But we can't get anywhere without a deeper look."

"But why didn't you say anything at the time, Louie—when we were all on board the ship?"

"We didn't want to confront Wolff openly. He obviously has a reason for keeping quiet about the code. If we mentioned that we'd encountered it, he might have done something rash."

Dana quelled a sense of mounting panic. Did the computer contain data about her parents or her sister? Was Jonathan lying about T. R. Edwards or the Invid? "Why are you coming to me with this?" she asked. "You should be talking to Jon—to Wolff."

Louie caught the slip and touched his chin. "I will talk to him—if you agree that that's the best way to proceed. See, I haven't mentioned anything about the code to Nova or Fredericks."

Dana was flustered. "What other way *is* there to proceed? If Wolff is the only one who can help you."

Louie dug the tip of his boot into the soft earth. "We're certain that the computer can be made permeable by a code word or a phrase. Granted, it has to be presented in Wolff's voice, but we can get around that." He glanced at Dana. "What we need first is the code."

It took Dana a moment to grasp his meaning. "You want me to pry the word out of him? Is that why you're here?"

Louie shrugged. "Like I said, I'll ask him directly if that's what you think's best."

Now Dana began to pace. "Why would he purposely conceal data about the REF or the Sentinels? He's already sick of being labeled a hero. If there's anything of worth in the ship's computer, he'd share it."

"Then why hasn't he told us about the voice code?"

Dana recalled his startled reaction to learning that the ship was to be surveyed. She put her hands over her mouth and shook her head.

"We have a second theory," Louie said quietly. "It's possible he's concealing that the ship is foldworthy." He raised his hands before Dana could speak. "The REF may have commanded him to return to Tirol once he had a clear picture of the situation here. He knows that he won't be allowed anywhere near that ship if the truth is revealed."

The words flattened her. Was that why Jonathan had claimed to believe so strongly in her vision—even though she hadn't mentioned anything about the ship? When they made love in his quarters on Denver Base, she had promised herself that she would have no expectations. She wasn't going to add to his confusion or further complicate his life. The physical intimacy they shared was only a prerequisite to intimacy of a different sort. If they were to be honest with one another about the future, that threshold would have to be crossed.

If there hadn't been an attraction, things might have gone differently. But neither of them could ignore what they felt, and they had acted on those feelings. Now, however, she had a clear and frightening understanding of the position she had put herself in, and she was hopelessly torn.

She screwed her eyes shut and continued to shake her head. "I don't know if I can do this for you, Louie. Things have gotten complicated . . ."

"Then do it for the Tiroleans," he said firmly. "If *The Homeward Bound* is foldworthy, it's their best shot at going home."

Dana balled up her hands. "That's low, Louie," she growled. "And cruel. If I refuse to pry the code out of him, I'm condemning everyone in camp to death, is that it?"

Louie showed her a sheepish look. "I'm sorry, Dana, I shouldn't have said that. Do whatever you think is right. Maybe if you tell him about the Tiroleans, he'll admit all he knows about the ship. Maybe the two of you can work out a deal. But if he says nothing about the code . . ." Louie shrugged.

Dana sat down on a stump and raised her face to the pine-scented breeze. Years earlier she had played the spy for Rolf by investigating the Giles Academy. But she had no stomach for espionage anymore. Couldn't she simply tell Jonathan that they knew all about the code? Then it would be up to him to decide whether or not to inform the GMP. Given the opportunity, would he return to Tirol? she wondered. To Lynn-Minmei and to all that he claimed to have run from? More to the point, if he chose to remain on Earth, would she be able to leave him—given the opportunity? Or would her concerns for the clones and for her parents overwhelm what *she* felt for him after only a few short weeks?

"Oh, Louie," she said, finally looking at him. "I wish you hadn't told me."

General Vincinz and his chiefs of staff were en route to the moon, aboard a twenty-year-old shuttle launched from Denver. At ALUCE, they were to meet with General Nobutu, to oversee the transfer of nuclear weapons to *The Homeward Bound* in advance of the Sensor Nebula mission. Weightlessness disagreed with Vincinz, though he enjoyed sending objects like pens and wristwatches wafting through the cabin space.

"Nova Satori's nobody's fool," he was telling the others just now. "When she came to me and casually dropped that little nugget about the Starchildren's plans to launch their ship, she knew from the start that I'd expect payment from the GMP if we were going to do their dirty work."

That dirty work had been carried out by a group of alleged Southern Cross deserters, who had gone to Argentina bearing gifts in the form of two fully armed A-JACs. The group was under orders to delay the launch, without inflicting damage on the ship itself, unless absolutely necessary. The mission couldn't be judged a complete success, inasmuch as two of the saboteurs had been captured and the ship had, in fact, sustained collateral damage in the fire that had spread from the targeted fuel dump. Nevertheless, not only was the ship grounded, but Vincinz could always claim to have done everything in his power to keep the Starchildren from suffering an irredeemable loss.

"I don't like the idea of Satori coming to us," Major Stamp said with candor. "Our willingness to execute the raid makes it appear that we have some special interest in protecting Wolff's ship."

Vincinz encouraged a piece of crumpled notepaper to drift from his open hand. "But that's the beauty of it. Of course we have a special interest in the ship. As the 'militant' faction of the retooled Defense Force, we are required to view *The Homeward Bound* as essential to Earth's survival in the face of an Invid onslaught. I practically said as much to Fredericks in the same casually meaningful tone Satori later used on me. That's how he got it in his head to use us in the first place."

"So what exactly do we get in exchange for grounding the Starchildren?" Captain Bortuk, the chief of staff, asked.

Vincinz held up two fingers. "First, unobstructed access to the data the Shimadas have promised to provide.

And second, Wolff's name is removed from the shortlist of candidates to command the Nebula mission."

"After the briefing he gave in Denver, there's a lot of people who would love to see him disappear," someone muttered.

"Wolff's a fool, thinking he can wage a guerrilla war against a bunch of XT slugs," Vincinz agreed. "Now more than ever, we need someone like Leonard at the helm. But it's imperative—especially now that Wolff's parade is being rained on—that he be kept away from the ship."

"Tokyo wants us to consider using their robots to man Wolff's ship for the run against the Sensor Nebula," Stamp supplied.

"Which isn't a half-bad idea," Vincinz replied, to everyone's surprise. "When the time comes to commandeer *The Homeward Bound*, it wouldn't hurt to have the help of a couple of smart machines that have already piloted her."

CHAPTER FOURTEEN

She would deny it to the last, but Sterling retains vestiges of the Imperative the Robotech Masters coded into the behavior of their warrior clones, the Zentraedi. In Sterling, however, the commingling of Human and Zentraedi genetics has twisted the Imperative into a willfulness, which masqueraded as precociousness in her infancy and toddlerhood, and rebelliousness in pubescence. I predict that, as she approaches full maturity, the Imperative will present in a more overt and dramatic fashion, overwhelming whatever codes of behavior to which she has hitherto adhered. In this sense, she is likely to be exceptionally impetuous, corruptible, manipulative, and self-serving. Though I hasten to add, this does not mean she should be exempted from active duty; to the contrary, she should be considered for high-risk undertakings whenever feasible, so as to encourage the surfacing of her warrior nature.

Lazlo Zand, *Event Horizon: Perspectives on Dana Sterling and the Second Robotech War*

"I'M WELL AWARE OF THE DANGERS POSED BY THIS mission," Senator Pauli told the members of the oversight committee. "But I consider it too important a mission to entrust to machines—no matter how allegedly intelligent they are." His gaze was focused on Louie Nichols. "You can tell the Shimadas, thanks, but no thanks. We've decided to go with a human crew on this one."

Louie adjusted the fit of his goggles. "I can appreciate that, Senator. But perhaps you'd be willing to allow one or two of the Shimada machines to participate as observers on the mission?"

Pauli looked to Aldershot, Grass, Fredericks, Satori, and the rest.

"I have no objections to allowing a robot to go along for the ride," Nova said. "Tokyo has been more than accommodating. There are potential military applications for some of the smart machines Shimada's people have designed. We may even be able to circumvent some of our reliance on Protoculture, vis-à-vis mecha power supply and reconfiguration."

Aldershot's adjutant, Major Sosa, was nodding in agreement. "I find it laudable that some of Tokyo's techs volunteered for the Nebula mission, even though we were constrained to reject the offers."

General Aldershot explained. "As long as Tokyo maintains its isolatory—and in some sense *collaborative*—stance with regard to the Invid, the Shimadas can't expect to be included in what is essentially a military operation. I will, however, tender my okay to the inclusion of a robot among the Nebula team—but only to serve as a redundant system to *The Homeward Bound*'s on-board computer."

"Exactly how much access to the on-board system will this machine have?" Senator Grass asked—as he had been instructed to by General Vincinz.

Louie answered for the Shimadas. "We're basically interested in evaluating the Nebula, Senator. In the event the nuclear devices fail to have the desired effect."

"So you're talking about having the robot serve as an additional sensor," Aldershot said.

Louie nodded. "I also think it couldn't hurt to have the machine evaluate the performance of the ship's Reflex furnaces. The more data we amass, the easier it's going to be to work toward revitalizing the Protoculture fold generators."

Aldershot considered it, then nodded in understanding. Louie was excused from the meeting. A vote was taken and the proposal was accepted.

"Have the fission bombs been transferred to the ship?" Pauli asked a moment later.

"General Vincinz confirms from ALUCE that we're a go," Nova told the table.

Pauli nodded approvingly. "Well, then, I suppose we need only arrive at a consensus as to our mission commander."

Grass cleared his throat. "I trust that by now we're all in agreement that Colonel Wolff and his officers and crew should be excluded?"

Fredericks and Nova traded covert glances. Payback time for Vincinz's actions in Argentina, Nova told herself.

"It makes good sense to keep Wolff out of it," Aldershot was saying. "The ship is similar enough in design to our existing frigates and destroyers to be piloted by any Southern Cross commander. And what with Wolff's experience in fighting the Invid, he's critical to our strategic posture."

"How's Wolff taking this?" Pauli put to Alan Fredericks.

Fredericks cleared his throat. "He hasn't been told. But his reaction shouldn't be a factor in our decision. Lang and Reinhardt sent him to help us, not contend with us."

"Then I agree with Senator Grass and General Aldershot that he be excluded," Pauli said, to a chorus of assenting voices.

Fredericks got to his feet with purposeful slowness. "The GMP submits that Dana Sterling is the best choice to oversee the mission."

"Sterling?" Pauli exclaimed. "She isn't even military personnel."

Fredericks inclined his head to one side. "It's true that her recent duties have had more to do with diplomacy than defense, but may I remind the committee that she has handled each assignment with competence and dedication to our common cause. She facilitated our growing rapport with Tokyo, she met with the Zentraedi—when we thought we had need of them—and she has already sat on the bridge of Wolff's ship. More importantly, Lieutenant Satori and I are in agreement that Sterling would meet with near universal approval. As former Southern Cross, she'll satisfy generals Vincinz and Nobutu; the Shimadas seem to have taken a liking to her; and we have reason to believe that even Wolff will support her."

Fredericks didn't need to look at Nova to guess what she was thinking. GMP operatives assigned to Wolff had reported that while Wolff may have encountered rough seas with his estranged wife and son, it had been nothing but smooth sailing with Dana Sterling.

"You make Sterling seem unassailable as a candidate, Colonel," Grass opined when Fredericks had finished. "But her actions during the War were often as reckless as they were heroic."

"That 'recklessness' has always paid off, Senator," Nova remarked. "Besides, there's one overriding reason for sending her."

Grass and the others waited.

"She's half Zentraedi," Nova said. "For all we know,

the Sensor Nebula may respond differently to her than it would to any of us. Perhaps, in addition to seeking out Flower of Life worlds, the Nebula also scans for the presence of enemies of the Invid."

The committee members spent a moment considering it.

"Yes, but based on the very reasons Colonel Fredericks gave for excluding Wolff," Pauli said at last, "can the Defense Force afford to lose Sterling?"

"We can't afford to lose anyone, Senator," Fredericks said, almost offhandedly. "But suffice it to say that we can afford to *risk* her."

Dana allowed herself to be swept into his embrace, and she returned the kisses he scattered across her lips, cheeks, and neck. But she broke it off when she felt her own passion begin to build. She couldn't make love to him now and do what she had to do. She refused to betray their intimacy in that way. She needed to confront him as honestly as possible and see what course he took.

"I've missed you," he whispered, reluctant to release her.

"I've missed you," she said, and slipped skillfully out of his arms.

His eyes were on her as she entered his quarters on Denver Base. "Have conditions improved at the cabin?" he asked after a moment.

She told him that there hadn't been any deaths since Bowie's alterations to the synthesizer, though neither Dana nor Musica expected their luck to hold. Then, sensing that it was as good a time as any to begin, she added, "A trip home is the only thing that can save them—a return to Tirol."

She watched him out of the corner of her eye, alert to every nuance in his expression. And indeed she identified a subtle rearrangement of his handsome features. It was as though a shadow had passed over his face. The light went out of his dark eyes. He exited the moment and went into himself. He was weighing something, gauging its import.

"I sympathize with what you're going through, Dana. I only wish there was something I could do." He followed her into the room, but walked past her, mumbling to himself. "Maybe, maybe there's a way . . ."

"What way, Jonathan? We both know the outcome. The clones will die, just as the Zentraedi did."

"If the ship could be retasked . . . I mean, if Louie or the Shimada team were to discover something about the fold generators."

Oh, but they have, she told herself, though she couldn't bring herself to give voice to the thought. So instead she said, "There's something I need to tell you, Jonathan. I wanted you to hear it from me first."

His fine brows beetled as he regarded her. "What, Dana?"

She straightened to her full height. "I've been asked to command the Nebula mission."

Wolff's eyes widened. *"What?"*

"That's why I'm back in Denver so soon," she said quickly. "Not that my heart has been anywhere but here. But command contacted me this morning, and ordered me to report."

Wolff couldn't control his consternation. When he turned to her, there was something new in his eye: a devilish ruefulness. "So they've taken my ship away from me."

She shook her head. "They haven't taken your ship. It's just that you're too valuable—"

"And you're not?" he snapped. "Earth's foremost celebrity? The half-XT soldier who practically ended the war single-handedly?"

"Jonathan—"

"I'm so valuable they don't even want me to waste my breath talking about the Invid." A sardonic laugh escaped him. "Don't you see what's behind this, Dana? They're worried I'm going to *leave*."

She swallowed hard. "But how could they think that? You've said all along that the ship isn't fold capable."

"No, no, of course it isn't," he answered in a distracted voice. "And here's the funny thing: I would have rejected the mission anyway. And you know why, Dana? Because I *am* too valuable. Or maybe I should say that my work comes first—ahead of anything the GMP or the Southern Cross can concoct."

"Your work?" she asked.

"My personal work." He put his hands in his pockets. "Actually, it's good they don't want to listen to me. Maybe they'll grant me a discharge. That way I'll be able to concentrate on what's important—getting over Lynn-Minmei and reconciling with my wife and son."

She stared at him. What was going on? It wasn't as if he was saying anything new, but he was saying it in a tone she hadn't heard him use before. An emphatic, almost accusative tone. Was he angry with her? Through with her? Or was he trying to tell her something? . . .

"I haven't accepted the mission," she started to tell him.

He whirled on her with such fury that it startled her. "But you have to accept it! You have to, do you understand me?"

She looked hard at him. "I have something else to tell you—something I haven't told anyone. When I met with the Zentraedi on the factory satellite, they informed me that our mission was a waste of time. There's no way to destroy the Sensor Nebula, Jonathan. And even if we manage to disrupt or disperse the cloud, it'll be too late. The Nebula has communicated with the Invid. They'll come, no matter what we do."

"It's not too late," he countered. "You're going to take the word of a group of dying Zentraedi? You have to accept the mission."

She exhaled in weary confusion. "Why couldn't Lang have surprised us by making the ship foldworthy—despite what he told you." Deliberately, she locked eyes with him.

He held her gaze for a protracted moment: uncertain, then angry, then sad. Finally he breathed deeply and smiled wanly, at once disappointed and relieved. "Imagine what a fool I'd look like," he said elaborately, "after insisting to everyone that *The Homeward Bound* was here to stay."

Dana tried hard to decipher his look and his words.

"But you're right," he went on, turning his back to her. "Lang shouldn't have sent me home with an imperfect ship. It's crucial that we communicate with the SDF-3. All of our efforts should be directed to that end. Vincinz and Aldershot have their minds made up about how to deal with the Regis, and it'll be the death of all of us."

"They don't want to surrender their authority to someone they see as a newcomer," Dana said in a low voice.

A smile flared on Wolff's face and died away. "Take good care of that ship, Dana," he said soberly. "It's Earth's only hope. Do you understand what I'm telling you? Use it as it was meant to be used. It's Earth's only hope, as surely as Lynn-Minmei was our hope during the Robotech War."

Again: Lynn-Minmei. Was he trying to hurt her? "Jonathan, you know that I would never do anything—"

"You can't be tied to me," he interrupted. "There's no room for sentiment in our lives. We all have separate parts to play, Dana. You know that as well as I do."

She tightened her lips and stared at the floor.

"You'd better go," he said, softening his tone. "There are preparations to make. Go now, Dana. Before it's too late."

In an aboveground laboratory in the Shimada Building, Miho Nagata watched Gibley, Shi Ling, and Strucker tinker with the disturbingly Humanlike robot that had been selected to ride *The Homeward Bound* into space. Reminiscent of the machines Emil Lang's staff of Robotechnicians had been experimenting with twenty years earlier and left to gather dust when Zand's Protoculture fiends inherited the facility, the plastic-sheathed thing had two legs, two arms, and a head, along with dozens of other appendages designed to gather and collate information. Gibley had told Nagata that the robot could see and hear from practically anywhere on its body.

"We have a pretty good idea of what happened in Argentina," Kan Shimada's number-one man was telling the trio as they worked. "The GMP somehow convinced General Vincinz to scuttle the launch of *Napperson's Hope*. The two women who were captured were former Southern Cross intelligence officers in Mexico."

"I'm surprised Vincinz was willing to cooperate," Gibley said in an offhand way, "after what Aldershot and Constanza have done to the Southern Cross. Why didn't the GMP handle it themselves?"

"Obviously they didn't want to compromise their intelligence agent." He smiled. "Our agent, I should say. She told them just enough to get them nervous, without revealing where the funding for the launch originated, so there are no ties to us."

Shi Ling peered at Nagata from behind the robot. "And the ship?" Gibley asked.

"Misa and our agent report that it was damaged, but apparently not irreparably so."

"Tough break," Strucker commented.

Miho nodded. "Mr. Shimada shares your concern. He feels that we are indirectly responsible for the damage, and has sent Terry back to Argentina to make amends."

Gibley secured a panel in the robot's thigh and stood up, stretching his arms over his head. "Is Kaaren Napperson planning to confront the Defense Force about the damage?"

"Her captives are denying any present affiliation with the Southern Cross," Nagata said. "They claim they were acting on behalf of the Heal Earth Hajj. Besides, Napperson knows better than to stir up further trouble."

A vid-phone chirped while everyone was mulling over Nagata's remarks, and Louie Nichols's face appeared onscreen a moment later.

"Lynn-Minmei," he said when Gibley had planted himself in front of the vid-phone camera.

"Uh, what's red and white, and irksome?" Gibley replied.

Louie forced a smile.

"Okay, I give up," Gibley said.

"Lynn-Minmei is *The Homeward Bound*'s voice-recognition code."

"You're kidding."

"No, and I doubt Dana is."

Shi Ling was suddenly at Gibley's side. "We'll have to scan the news-footage files to see if we've got audio of Wolff saying her name."

Louie shook his head. "Won't be necessary." He held up a minidisk. "Dana wired herself."

CHAPTER
FIFTEEN

A glance at the events that transpired between the [Second and Third Robotech] wars is likely to leave one with the impression that the actual function of the Invid Sensor Nebula was to so confound the inhabitants of Earth that they would be incapable of taking any action that might deflect or otherwise repel the swarm. Given the conduct of the revamped government, the dismantled Southern Cross, the impotent Defense Force, the orchestrating Shimada Family, the naïve Starchildren, and the foundering 15th ATAC, one is tempted to view Leonard, Moran, even Zand in a more benevolent light.

Selig Kahler, *The Tirolean Campaign*

THIS TIME WHEN SATORI AND FREDERICKS ARRIVED AT the refugee camp, they found the barbwire-crowned gate wide open. Dana, Bowie, Angelo, and Sean were waiting for them, on the ground rather than inside the battered Hovertanks they had salvaged from the war-torn streets of Monument City. Groups of Tirolean refugees watched warily from the Emerson cabin, the watchtowers, and the deep shadows of fir trees. Musica stood off to one side of the gate, cradling the clone infant in her arms.

"You'd better have a damn good reason for making us come all the way from Denver," Fredericks said to Dana, in the affected tone that had endeared him to no one.

Dana stood akimbo. "I'll let you be the judge of that, Colonel."

The former members of the 15th led the climb up the grassy slope to a large field, strewn with graves, marked only by knee-high piles of river-smoothed stones. The desiccated, overturned earth was the color of cocoa.

"On the Masters' mother ships, clones that died or were determined to be defective were simply recycled," Bowie told the two GMP officers. "But since we lack the technology for that, and because cremation is for some reason anathema to the Tiroleans, it was either interment or cryogenic preservation. As you can see, we chose burial."

Nova's eyes were larger than usual as they roamed the field. "My God, how many have died?"

"One hundred and three," Angelo said gruffly.

"If you'd surrendered them to our custody . . ." Fredericks started to say, only to be cut off by Sean.

"They would have died anyway."

Nova had a hand over her mouth. "Surely we can get a medical team to come up here . . ."

But Dana was shaking her head. "It's too late for that, Nova. Anyway, we've already treated the ones who came down with diseases. What you see here is mainly the result of madness and malnutrition. The war was even tougher on them than it was on us, and now, everything about the place is killing them: the air, the openness, the food . . . They have to be moved to a secure environment where they can tend to their own healing. And they require special nutrients we can't supply, because we've run out of downed assault ships to plunder."

"Dana, I don't know what you expect us to do," Nova said.

"I'll tell you what I expect." Dana took a couple of

steps toward them. "I need your help in transferring them to the factory satellite."

Fredericks snorted in disbelief. "While the *Zentraedi* are on board? Are you certain you've thought this through, Sterling?"

"The Zentraedi have more in common with these people than they do with us," Dana told him. "Their gripes were with the Masters, not the clones the Masters created. They'll accept the Tiroleans. More importantly, the factory's life-support system is still producing a synth food that contains the Protoculture chemicals that are indispensable to their health."

Nova blew out her breath. "We don't have the authority to facilitate an operation of this scope."

"I know that, Nova. But I need you to act as our intermediary with Aldershot and Constanza and whomever else. Tell them that we want three shuttles. They're to be delivered to what's left of Fokker Base, and launched from there, as well. I'll pilot one; Sean will pilot the second; and I want Marie Crystal to pilot the third. We'll see to getting the Tiroleans aboard and lofting them to the factory satellite. We won't require any escorts, and we want full clearance to carry out the debarking of our passengers without interference. From the factory, we will proceed directly to *The Homeward Bound*."

Fredericks curled his lip at her. "This is beginning to sound like blackmail, Sterling."

Dana almost grinned. "My—or I should say, *our*—acceptance of the Nebula mission is contingent on it. Unless our terms are met, Aldershot and the lot of them can find another crew for Wolff's ship."

Nova gnawed her lower lip. "Dana, before you issue

any further ultimatums, I should caution you: There are other qualified candidates."

Dana nodded. "But you people owe me this much. For my acting as your emissary to Tokyo and the factory-satellite Zentraedi ... And every day you delay costs all of us. Tell that to Constanza and Aldershot, Nova. And advise them that we're ready to go at a moment's notice."

"I can't say I'm any more comfortable with this than I am with weightlessness," Vincinz announced, surveying his roomy subsurface quarters on ALUCE Base, "but it does feel good to be within fifty thousand miles of our prize."

The Homeward Bound, Vincinz meant, which he and some of the others had been briefly aboard during the transfer of the fission bombs. And a fine ship she was, he had told himself at the time. Somewhat cramped and unfinished, but suitable for spearheading an attack on the Invid. Or for spacefolding to Tirol—once Shimada's team had finished working their Protoculture magic.

With Vincinz were his adjutant, his chief of staff, and two Southern Cross captains who were loyal to Vincinz but had spent the past two months attached to General Nobutu's command. A lanky, long-haired TASC lieutenant named Lancer had shown everyone to Vincinz's quarters and had promised to have the kitchen deliver food and drink.

Major Stamp pounded his hand against the room's arc of alloy wall, as if testing its strength. "Tell you the truth, I think I'd rather be here than on Earth if and when the Invid come. Especially if Wolff turns out to be right about their ignoring the moon."

"Do you want to wait around and see if he's right?" Vincinz asked.

"I only meant—"

"I know what you meant. But I anticipate we'll be on our way within a couple of weeks. As I see it, Sterling's mission to the Nebula will provide those Tokyo *otaku* with everything they need to run a full assessment of the fold generators. It'll just be a matter of time before they announce that the ship's already foldworthy or that they can make it so."

"Sterling," Captain Bortuk remarked with patent distaste. "Who would have figured a *Zentraedi* going mushy over a bunch of clones."

Vincinz snorted. "Anyone who fought with Sterling during the war. She was the first one to protest the wholesale slaughter of Bioroid pilots because they were *Human*."

"The younger generation," one of the captains said. "Too bad she wasn't around to see what Humans were doing to Humans during the Global Civil War."

"Still, going to the trouble to loft them to the factory satellite . . ."

"All we need now are some Invid, and we'll have ourselves a regular XT petting zoo," Stamp added, laughing at his own joke.

They were all laughing when Lancer, the fly-boy, reappeared at the door. "General Vincinz, high-priority commo from Senator Grass." He gestured to the room's communications terminal. "The encryption is unfamiliar to us, sir."

"I'll see to it, Lieutenant," Vincinz said, dismissing him. Then, prizing a hand-held computer from the breast pocket of his jacket, he went to the terminal and downloaded Grass's message. A moment later, he had the hand-held on-line with a stand-alone CRT monitor, and everyone was huddled around it.

Grass was seated at his desk in the Denver building the resurrected UEG was leasing from a produce supplier.

"General Vincinz: Stop right now if you haven't taken the necessary precautions." Grass paused for several seconds, then began again. "Ever since it was learned that Starchildren had set a launch date for *Napperson's Hope*, the GMP has been following the money that financed the rapid readying of the ship. It appears now that the funds originated in Tokyo, and also that the *Shimadas* may have had their sights set on Wolff's ship.

"The conclusion being drawn down here is that they know more about that ship than they've let on. Which begs the question: Have they shared what they know with anyone else? Get back to me as soon as possible, Vincinz. I don't want to be left on Earth if the balloon goes up ahead of schedule."

Vincinz turned to Stamp. "When is Sterling slated to loft the clones to the factory satellite?"

"Today. Oh-six-hundred hours, Denver time."

Vincinz consulted his wrist watch. "That gives us just under twelve hours."

"To do what, sir?"

"To beat Sterling to *The Homeward Bound*. That ship isn't going anywhere without us."

Nova, Fredericks, and three other GMP officers had a room to themselves in Denver Base's mission-control complex. Dana's shuttle convoy was up and away—in spite of a few last-minute problems at Fokker Aerospace—and the three ships were being tracked and monitored. All of Dana's terms had been met: the UEG had okayed the demand that her crew be made up of the former members of the 15th ATAC, in addition to Lieutenant Marie Crystal of the Black Lions TASC squadron; the Tiroleans were cleared for transfer to the factory satellite; and the 15th was authorized to proceed directly to *The Homeward Bound* and commence countdown for the Nebula mission.

Although there were far fewer display screens, the room the GMP officers had to themselves received the same data that was being relayed to the central control room. Just now, most of the monitors were displaying video feeds from the pilot cabins of the three shuttles. There were Sean and Bowie; Angelo and Marie; and, in the third and largest shuttle, Dana, partnered with the Shimadas' somewhat grotesque, Humaniform robot, and some silly-looking, poodlelike stuffed animal Dana had brought along. But while Fredericks and the other officers were regarding the screens, Nova was listening— via audio earbeads—to a recording of a conversation Wolff and Sterling had had, ten days earlier, in Wolff's quarters.

There's no way to destroy the Sensor Nebula, Jonathan, Dana had said to him at one point. *And even if we manage to disrupt or disperse the cloud, it'll be too late. The Nebula has communicated with the Invid. They'll come, no matter what we do.*

That Dana had heard as much from the factory-satellite Zentraedi and had failed to report it might have been grounds for bouncing her from the Nebula mission. But Nova had decided not to bring the recording to the attention of the oversight committee. Her personal beliefs notwithstanding, Dana could claim to have simply dismissed the information, on the assumption that the Zentraedi were frequently misinformed about tactical data—a claim that would be backed up by her acceptance of the mission.

It's not too late, Wolff had told her. *You have to accept the mission.*

Nova was unclear as to why she had become preoccupied with the recording. However, because the onset of that preoccupation had coincided with the arrival of new intelligence about the Starchildren, she sensed that she was searching for a clandestine link between the Shimadas and Wolff, or perhaps between the Shimadas and Dana.

The funds that were to have financed the launch of *Napperson's Hope* had been traced to Tokyo. Behind Fredericks's back, Nova had authorized a payment of $500,000 to their informant, and the woman had spilled what she knew about the Shimada connection.

As Sterling herself had helped to establish, the Shimadas claimed to have no interest in either abandoning the elegant underground empire they had forged, or contributing to the refurbishment of Earth's decimated Defense Force. Rather, they had hopes of accommodating the Invid with the aliens' own Flowers of Life, like some antiwar hippie crusade from the previous century. It followed, then, that they might have viewed Wolff's ship as a threat to their plans, and had therefore attempted to arrange for its destruction or disappearance—at the hands of the Starchildren or who knew what other groups.

All of which would have been well and good, save

for one piece of intelligence that had also come to light: the GMP operative had stated that the person who had supplied the information about the Starchildren's launch was Terry Weston—*a Shimada subordinate*.

That being the case, what had happened to compel the Shimadas to reverse the plan they had set in motion? Never mind that they had manipulated the GMP and the Southern Cross to achieve their ends; had they discovered a better way of disposing of the ship?

Nova paused the playback of the recordings to study the monitor screens. Sean and Bowie, Angelo and Marie, Dana and the robot . . .

The two-legged machine had been scanned and probed, and declared to be essentially harmless. It wasn't harboring a bomb or any program that could initialize a self-destruct sequence in Wolff's ship. As desperate as the Shimadas might be to rid the planet of *The Homeward Bound*, it was unlikely that they would knowingly sacrifice Dana and her crew in the process.

So what wasn't she seeing?

She studied the display screens some more, finding her attention drawn again to the wide-angle feed from the shuttle Dana piloted. The Shimada bot's tinted vision array suddenly brought Louie Nichols to mind, and Nova laughed at the comparison. But her amusement faltered almost immediately, and she hurriedly commanded the Sterling/Wolff conversation to recommence play.

Why couldn't Lang have surprised us by making the ship foldworthy, Dana had mused *despite what he told you.*

Nova fast-forwarded through the initial portion of Wolff's reply. "*. . . Lang shouldn't have sent me home in an imperfect ship. It's crucial that we communicate* *with the SDF-3. All of our efforts should be directed to that end."* Again, she fast-forwarded. *"Take good care of that ship, Dana. It's Earth's only hope. Do you understand what I'm telling you? Use it as it was meant to be used. It's Earth's only hope . . ."*

Nova didn't have to run the recording through a voice analyzer to know that Wolff's statements were informed by a subtext. Clearly, he had realized that the GMP had him under surveillance.

Use the ship as it was meant to be used . . .

How was it "meant" to be used? Hadn't it, in fact, already discharged its importance by returning Wolff and his Pack to Earth? Or did it have a secondary objective to fulfill that had nothing to do with the Nebula mission?

Why couldn't Lang have made the ship foldworthy? Had he?

Did Wolff know, and had the Shimadas found out?

Nova cut her eyes to the display screens.

The robot!

She reached for the phone and barked, "Patch me though to General Aldershot—highest priority!"

It was a moment before the operator got back to her. "I'm sorry, sir, but the general can't be disturbed."

"He can't be *disturbed*? Did you tell him that this was highest priority, Corporal?"

"Affirmative, sir. But a situation has developed at ALUCE—"

"What situation?"

"Sir, General Vincinz and his chiefs of staff have departed unexpectedly from ALUCE in a commandeered frigate, and are apparently en route to *The Homeward Bound.*"

CHAPTER SIXTEEN

Sterling never explained how the "cha-cha," the pollinator she called Polly—a gift from her three Zentraedi godfathers—reached Tirol. All the principals in the pre-War drama surrounding The Homeward Bound *reported that the pollinator was not aboard the shuttles, or the ship itself, and Sterling herself has denied Satori's claim that she observed it during her surveillance of Sterling's flight to the factory satellite—though apparently mistook it for a stuffed toy poodle. Several commentators have argued that, in fact, it wasn't Polly who followed Sterling out of the Tirol-arrived* Homeward Bound, *but one of the many cha-chas that were known to have resided in captivity in Tiresia when the REF captured the city from the Invid Regent. [See La Paz, Baker, Huxley, and others.] It's possible that Polly was overlooked during the boarding of the shuttles, the flight to Wolff's ship, and the relatively brief fold to Tirol. But, then, how is it the little, knob-horned, mopheaded creature was glimpsed by numerous foragers who descended on the Emerson cabin* after *the departure of Sterling, Grant, Dante, Phillips, and the Tirolean refugees?*

Mari Peirce, *Homeward Bound*

REPAIRS TO THE IRIS GATE OF THE FACTORY SATELlite's three o'clock pod had been completed a week earlier, but two small work ships were still anchored to the rotating factory when the convoy of shuttles approached. While the repairs were being effected, there had been sporadic radio contact between the work vessels and the Zentraedi, but neither crew members nor technicians had ventured any deeper into the factory than the docking bay of the enormous pod itself.

Dana, too, had spoken briefly with Tay Wav'vir—the

domillan—and Tay had promised to be on hand when Dana arrived. Dana hadn't apprised her of the purpose of the visit; though, what with the trio of shuttles, the Zentraedi were likely to surmise that their earlier request for mecha and weapons had been granted.

The shuttles negotiated the iris gate in single file, entering the vast forlorn chamber Dana had last visited in an EVA rig. When the shuttles had powered down, she emerged from the shuttle's forward doorway accompanied by three nearly identical female Tiroleans, who together formed a Triumvirate. All were wearing flight suits.

Waiting in the bay were Tay Wav'vir and the seventy-five or so other females, looking even more haggard than they had scarcely two months earlier.

"*Par dessu*, Daughter of Parino," the purple-haired Tay announced. "We were beginning to wonder if we would ever set eyes on you again."

"There's been much to attend to," Dana said.

Tay smirked. "Have your superiors abandoned their plans to assault the Sensor Nebula, or will they use the Super Dimensional Fortress that recently arrived?"

"Is it truly an REF ship?" someone asked before Dana could reply.

Dana nodded to the Zentraedi who had spoken. "Colonel Wolff, the commander, is an REF officer."

"Colonel Jonathan Wolff?" someone else asked.

"Jonathan Wolff, yes."

The Zentraedi turned to her closest comrades. "The malcontent exterminator," she said. "Leader of the Wolff Pack."

The statements elicited an excited murmuring among some of the Zentraedi. This briefly overpowered a wary muttering that had begun in another quarter, and was clearly directed at the Triumvirate. After a thickly built female from the latter group said something in confidence to Tay Wav'vir, the *domillan* cut her eyes to the triplets and uttered several phrases in Zentraedi.

Nonplussed, the Tiroleans looked to Dana, who had anticipated the Zentraedi's reaction. "They are not T'sentrati," she said when the separate conversations had quieted. "They are from Tirol. Aboard the shuttles are an additional hundred."

Tay held up her hands to silence everyone. "What is your purpose in bringing them here, Daughter of Parino?"

"I'm taking them home, *Domillan* Wav'vir. And I've come to ask you to join us."

Bafflement clouded Tay's eyes. "Home?"

"To Tirol," Dana said. "I can't provide you with the weapons you requested, but I can at least offer you a chance to return to your home space along with them."

Isolated sniggering punctuated the stunned silence.

"Tirol is not our home," Tay explained, in a somewhat amused voice. "Most of us on this station have never even seen *Fantoma*, let alone made planetfall on its inhabited moon. If Tirol meant anything to us, we would have shipped aboard the SDF-3 all those years ago." She glanced disdainfully at the Triumvirate. "Tirol may hold significance for these clones the Masters created to populate their empire, but the moon holds no significance for us."

Dana had not anticipated this. "Would you stay here, then, in this dead thing, with the Invid on the approach?"

"This dead thing is as much a home as we have ever

known," someone replied. "That's why we sued for permission to defend it."

"But monumental changes have occurred in Tirolspace," Dana said. "Lord Breetai commands his own ship once more: the *Valivarre*, fueled by ore freshly mined from Fantoma. And the forces of the Regent have been driven off Karbarra, Praxis, Garuda, Spheris, and many other worlds. This is the dawn of a new era—an era in which the T'sentrati can participate, not as enslaved warriors, but as an autonomous people."

Tay Wav'vir heard her out, then turned to her confederates. "Step forward, without fear of dishonor, any who would leave this place."

But no one made a move.

"Hey, you can't go in there," Aldershot's aide shouted to Nova as she stormed past his desk.

"The hell I can't," Nova said under her breath.

After numerous attempts to reach Aldershot from mission control, she had finally left Fredericks to mind the store and sped over to Denver Base in a borrowed Jeep, barely avoiding accidents on three occasions.

"Satori! What in blazes—" Aldershot's adjutant said as she came through the office door with the aide hot on her heels.

The general himself, surrounded by several officers and technical specialists, was seated in front of an array of monitors, some of which were displaying views of the frigate Vincinz had apparently hijacked from ALUCE. Aldershot turned when he heard the commotion and waved his aide and Major Sosa off Nova as they were trying to hustle her from the room.

Nova gave a downward tug to her tunic, flipped her

hair behind her shoulders, and saluted. "I'm sorry to break in like this, General, but no one would put me through to you."

Aldershot scowled. "Excuse us, Lieutenant, if we were too busy dealing with a mutiny to return your calls."

"But, sir, it may not be a mutiny. If you'll give me a minute to explain what I've learned about the Shimadas—"

"The Shimadas and their secret-agent robot," Aldershot interrupted. "I've taken your conjectures under advisement, and if there's anything to them, action will be taken at the appropriate time."

"But *now* is the appropriate time," Nova replied forcefully. "The Shimadas are planning to fold *The Homeward Bound* to Tirol."

Everyone in the room turned to her.

"It's fold capable, sir," she went on. "Wolff knew this from the start, and the Tokyo team found him out. I can't make a case for conspiracy—not at the moment, anyway—but I'm certain that the Shimadas have incorporated the spacefold codes into their robot." She paused, then added. "The Shimadas' machine is going to take control of the ship."

Aldershot showed her a look of angry disbelief.

"And just why would Tokyo want to do such a thing?" the chief of staff asked in a patronizing voice.

Nova steeled herself. "They want the ship to disappear. They don't care where it goes, or if it takes another five years to get there. They want it away from Earth, so we'll have nothing substantial to hurl against the Invid when they arrive."

After a long moment, Aldershot spoke. "Ms. Satori,

that's the most preposterous assumption I've heard in some time. You and Colonel Fredericks have been so busy chasing phantoms that you overlooked the plot that was hatching right under your noses. General Vincinz and his staff are the ones we need to be concerned about—not a bunch of *yakuza* and their two-legged computer."

"But, sir—"

The general held up his hands. "No more buts." He gestured to one of the monitors. "See for yourself, Lieutenant: Vincinz is headed for *The Homeward Bound*. Fortunately, we learned of his treachery in time to divert the shuttle rendezvous squadron to intercept him."

Nova turned her attention to a monitor that showed several Logans closing on the frigate. "Have you asked yourself what Vincinz is planning to do once he gets aboard Wolff's ship?" she asked Aldershot. "If you recall, sir, he and the rest of the Southern Cross staff officers okayed the mission. Why would they take such drastic measures to thwart it, unless they had good reasons to be suspicious?"

Major Sosa snorted in derision. "Ask yourself why Vincinz failed to alert us to those 'good reasons,' Satori. For God's sake, he won't even respond to our hailings."

Nova met his look. "Perhaps he didn't think *you'd* listen to reason."

Sosa had his mouth open to reply when one of the techs reported that the Logans were within targeting range of the frigate.

"Tell the pilots to continue hailing the ship," Aldershot ordered. "They are not to go to guns unless they find themselves in laser lock." He looked over his shoulder at Nova. "General Vincinz knows that *The

Homeward Bound is the only effective weapon we have at our disposal, and he doesn't trust that we'll make proper use of it. He's indignant that we were given custody of the ship, and he wants it back. It's as simple as that, Lieutenant."

Nova worked her jaw. "May I speak candidly, sir?"

"Candidly, but briefly."

"Sir, I feel that you're allowing yourself to be blinded by old rivalries between the Southern Cross and the RDF. Vincinz means to commandeer *The Homeward Bound* because he has somehow learned what I have: that the Shimadas have only their own agenda. You've got to let him reach that ship, General. Even if he commandeers it, he won't be able to execute a spacefold without the necessary codes. And even if I'm completely wrong, we can always retake the ship if Vincinz refuses to surrender it. He's not about to fire on his own forces."

"General Aldershot," a tech said. "Black Lions Five and Six report that they are being targeted by the frigate. They are taking evasive action."

Everyone turned to the monitors, where, on one screen, two Logans were veering from their courses. An instant later, a burst of cyan light erupted from the starboard guns of the frigate, missing the mecha by a narrow mark.

Aldershot muttered a curse. "Still no response from Vincinz?"

"None, sir."

"Then it's done," the general said wearily. "Order the squadron to cripple that ship."

* * *

In Black Lion Two, Dennis Brown rolled away from the frigate, then angled beneath her, out of harm's way for the moment. Five and Six had nearly been scorched by the starboard laser array, and the tactical net was noisy with chatter.

"Talk isn't going to stop that ship," Dennis suggested good-naturedly.

"Sorry, Two," Five said, "but I was one of Vincinz's aides, so I'm a bit freaked that he'd try to dust me."

"Maybe that's why he's trying to dust you," Three said.

Dennis thought about Nova, listening to the remarks over the command net, and decided to get serious. "I'm pretty well positioned to stitch the aft power plant," he told his wingmate.

"Go for it, Two. Nothing fancy. And keep it clean."

"Roger that, One. No Fokker feints."

Dennis cut his forward speed, falling back until the tail end of the frigate was directly overhead. If Vincinz was going to burn him, it would be now. But the escort's underbelly guns didn't traverse. No one laser locked him.

"Sitting duck," he said into his helmet mouthpiece, and loosed a gaggle of Mongooses.

"Our wings have been clipped," Captain Bortuk reported from his post on the bridge of the hijacked frigate. "Principal drives are down. We're dead in space."

"Traitors!" General Vincinz snarled through barred teeth, struggling against the grip of the two officers who had dragged him away from the weapons console before he could loose a second blast at the Logan pursuit team.

Major Stamp swung his chair through a half circle. "You're the traitor, Vincinz. Firing on our own people."

Vincinz glowered. "Did you have some other way of reaching the ship with them in our way?"

Stamp rose and approached Vincinz. "If we'd made it by stealth it would be one thing. But I'm not about to kill innocent people. And unless I'm sorely mistaken, General, your stunt may have cost us our only alibi."

"Sir, General Aldershot is hailing on the command frequency," their communications man said.

Stamp blew out his breath. "No one is to speak but me, is that understood? I'm going to play this as close to the vest as I can." He slipped into the command chair, composed himself for the camera, and nodded to the commo man. "Put him through."

Aldershot appeared on one of the heads-up screens, distorted by intermittent static. Seeing Stamp in the driver's seat, he said, "Where's Vincinz?"

"General Vincinz has been temporarily relieved of duty. I don't expect you to believe this, Aldershot, but our burst was unintentional."

"As was your hijacking that frigate, I suppose."

"Not entirely, no."

Aldershot snorted. "Do you want to explain your actions now, or save it for the inquest and court-martial?"

Stamp wet his lips. "The truth is that we've come into some information that may well endanger the Nebula mission."

Aldershot blinked and was silent for a moment. "What sort of information, Major?"

"That Tokyo didn't reveal all they discovered about the capacities of *The Homeward Bound*."

"And why wasn't the GMP or the oversight committee apprised of this?

"To be blunt, we didn't think we'd be listened to. A lot of what we have on the Shimadas is circumstantial, and we couldn't be sure of presenting sufficient hard evidence to delay the mission."

"That was damn foolish of you, Major."

"We were well aware of the risks. But we felt obliged to give it our best shot."

"You damn fools!" Vincinz shouted from behind the command chair. "That ship is going to jump, Aldershot, and you're going to have to live with the consequences!"

Aldershot narrowed his eyes. "Put Vincinz where I can see him."

Vincinz shrugged his captors off and planted himself directly in front of his adjutant. "Listen to me, Aldershot: There wasn't time to consult you or to request Nobutu's permission to borrow this ship. We had to act fast and trust that we were doing the prudent thing."

"I hardly consider targeting the pursuit team the prudent thing," Aldershot told him. "And I'm not convinced that your burst was accidental. This is the same battle we've been fighting for twelve years, Vincinz: Southern Cross against Robotech. You're lucky I didn't order those Logans to pick you apart."

"We'll see who's 'lucky,' Aldershot—at the inquest, as you say."

Aldershot started to reply when one of his staff passed him a slip of paper. His face was ashen when he looked into the camera.

Vincinz and the others aboard the bridge strained to

make out what was being said two hundred thousand miles away. Then Aldershot cleared his throat.

"I've just been informed by the pilot of one of the Logans still positioned at the shuttle rendezvous point that Commander Sterling appears to have taken the Tiroleans with her. The sentries have been overpowered, and Sterling is in the process of relocating the clones aboard *The Homeward Bound*."

Vincinz let out a rueful laugh. "She's folding to Tirol, you old fool! That damned half-breed is out of here!"

The view from the forward bays encompassed all that had been her life for eighteen years: Space Station Liberty, the factory satellite, cold Luna, and wounded Earth. While Sean, Marie, and Angelo were strapping into their seats and bringing *The Homeward Bound*'s systems on-line, Dana peered into her past and tried to imagine her future.

Bowie and Musica were elsewhere in the ship, seeking out sheltered places for their hundred Tirolean passengers, and the TASC guards had been disarmed and transferred to the abandoned shuttles. The Shimadas' robot was at the rear of the bridge, mated to a wall of technology by means of a pencil-thin connector that projected from the front of its alloy thorax. A pale lavender light glowed behind its wraparound vision array.

At Fokker Base, during preflight—and in the moments before a visual feed had been established with mission control in Denver—Louie had spoken to Dana through the robot, which had been delivered to Monument by a Shimada security team.

"The machine will see to everything, Dana. Just show it to the computer link on the bridge and task it to in-

terface. When you're ready to execute the fold, tell the machine to initialize the Protoculture generators.

"Oh, and by the way, we figured out where Lang went wrong. Your fold to Tirol should be near instantaneous. The machine contains a download of our calculations, including all my notes relating to the Synchron drive. I hope Lang and Penn can make sense of them. But be sure to tell them of the part that Tokyo played in getting you there—I figure this is Kan Shimada's way of ingratiating himself with the REF in advance of the fleet's return to Earth. Now if we can just weather the Invid Storm . . .

"Don't feel that you're abandoning us in our hour of need, Dana. Just keep in mind what you felt after the Masters were defeated. You knew then that this would be your destiny, just as you knew that Tokyo would be mine. I speak for all of us in the underground in telling you to 'Hurry back.' "

Dana had been given a glimpse of her destiny aboard the Master's flagship, and she had been watching it unfold ever since, playing an active part in that unfolding and refusing to credit any of it to the "Shapings" of Protoculture or any other metaphysical agency. She felt more clearheaded and resolute than she had ever felt, despite the ruggedness of the moral terrain she was traversing. Louie and the Shimada Family didn't view her departure as abandonment, but many would. Her actions during the war would be forgotten. She would be seen as a coward of the worst sort. And yet, was there any other path open to her? One that would not only take into account the Tiroleans and the Shimadas, but would speak to Earth's still-questionable future?

Part of her wanted to steer a course for the Sensor

Nebula and make it appear as if *The Homeward Bound* succumbed to destructive forces. But she couldn't bring herself to slip away like that, on a calculated lie.

And, of course, there was Jonathan.

She may have glimpsed his ship in her premonition, but she hadn't glimpsed him, or foreseen the cruel dance of circumstance that would engulf both of them. He had sanctioned her treason, just as Emil Lang must have sanctioned Jonathan's when he had hijacked a ship to deliver to the derelict Sentinels. And he had sanctioned her abandoning him, by telling her that she couldn't be tied to him; that there was no room for sentiment in their lives; that they each had their parts to play—

"Dana," Sean said suddenly. "Highest priority commo from Denver Base."

She turned from the view. "Let's hear it."

Nova Satori's cool voice issued from the speakers. "Dana, this is Nova. I'm with General Aldershot. We are delaying the mission. Repeat: we are delaying the mission. Do you copy, Dana? Please respond."

Dana signaled Angelo to open an audio channel. "We copy, Denver. But we strongly urge that you reconsider. That Sensor Nebula is waiting, and we don't want to miss our launch window."

Nova didn't reply immediately, and when she did her voice was heavy with disappointment. "Dana, we know that you've brought the Tiroleans aboard, and we have reason to suspect that the Sensor Nebula isn't tops on your list of places to go."

Dana and Sean exchanged defeated glances. "Denver," Dana said, "the Zentraedi wouldn't accept the clones. I had no choice but to transfer them."

Aldershot answered her in a firm voice. "It won't work, Sterling. It seems that that ship is foldworthy, after all. And some of us feel that you mean to fold it to Tirol."

Dana took a moment to compose her thoughts, then forced a slow exhale. "You're correct, General—on both counts."

"Dana—"

"You're wasting your breath, Nova. Colonel Wolff didn't realize the ship was fold capable, but the Tokyo team learned the truth—"

"I don't believe that for a minute," Nova interjected.

Dana raised her voice. "Lang programmed the ship's on-board computers to time-release the fold codes three months from now. But Shimada's team persuaded the computer to divulge the codes ahead of time."

"You can't do this to us, Dana."

"Sterling, I am ordering you to surrender the ship."

"I'm sorry, sir," Dana said. "I can't do that."

"For a hundred Tirolean clones?" Nova asked in distress.

"You're a traitor to your people, Sterling."

Dana swallowed hard and found her voice. "I'll accept that, sir. But we all have our parts to play, our separate destinies to fulfill. To begin with, there's no destroying the Nebula. The Zentraedi assured me that it couldn't be done. The Invid are coming, and—despite what Vincinz thinks—the presence of this ship isn't going to make much of a difference, one way or the other. In fact, Earth's probably better off without it."

"You've been corrupted by those damned *yakuza*," Aldershot growled.

"Think what you will. But someone has to communicate with the REF, and it might as well be me. And all the better if a hundred displaced Tiroleans are returned to their home planet at the same time."

"Quit trying to justify your treachery, Sterling."

"Time will tell if I've taken the right course, sir. I hope we're able to sit down and discuss this episode a year or so from now, when I return with the SDF-3 and enough troops to send the Invid back where they came from. But until then, I suggest you listen to Colonel Wolff and give the Regis what she wants."

"Don't expect me *ever* to sit down with you, Sterling."

Dana shut her eyes and signaled Angelo to mute the audio feed. "Are we ready?" she asked Sean.

"Almost. Just want to put a bit more distance between us and the shuttles."

"No hitchhiking allowed," Marie said.

Dana settled into the command chair, enabled the restraints, and moved her gaze from Marie to Angelo to Sean. "Any last minute regrets?" she asked.

After the head shaking was done, Dana turned to the robot. "Machine: initialize the Protoculture generators."

In Jonathan Wolff's voice, the robot said, "Lynn-Minmei," and *The Homeward Bound* gave a protracted shudder, powered up, and disappeared from sight.

CHAPTER SEVENTEEN

*Despite everything we'd been through, I couldn't help but feel
sorry for him, because I knew how driven he was. Or, a better
way to put that is that I knew, I understood what drove him. I
don't think that people set out to be heroes; heroes surface from
circumstances that are often beyond their control. My husband
had a need to be in that zone—where events teetered on
disorder—because it was only then that he could tap his real
strengths, as a man, as a Human being. Perhaps that's why he
was his most loving when things between us were most chaotic. I
can't account for his alleged betrayal at the end, his conspiring
[sic] with the Invid [See Rand, Notes on the Run], except to say
that he must have been biding his time, waiting for the right opportunity to strike. I don't feel that it had anything to do with my
and Johnny's captivity. If he had been with us in Albuquerque instead of in Valhalla, he would simply have been taken prisoner
along with the rest of us. So, no, I don't hold him responsible, and
I pray that he didn't hold himself responsible. We were two
people, Johnny and I, and poor Jonathan felt that he had an entire world to rescue.*

Catherine Montand Wolff, as quoted in Zeus Bellow's
The Road to Reflex Point

IT WAS TIROL ALL OVER AGAIN, WOLFF TOLD HIMSELF
while Eiten Shimada read a prepared statement for the
tribunal.

"Furthermore, Shimada Enterprises denies any fore-
knowledge regarding or related to the capacities and ca-
pabilities of the star ship known as *The Homeward
Bound*. As previously stated, the smart machine that accompanied the flight crew was designed merely to evaluate the vessel's performance and to serve as a

redundant system in analyzing the effect of the fission bombs on the Sensor Nebula cloud.

"Lieutenant Sterling's statement to the effect that technicians in the employ of Shimada Enterprises discovered a key to the operation of the ship's spacefold system has no basis in fact. Moreover, it has yet to be demonstrated that Shimada Enterprises was anything but charitable in this entire matter. The robot and other examples of Shimada technology were provided to the Defense Force freely and without expectation of recompense. It is therefore the decision of President Misui and the other members of the Diet, along with those named by the court, that these proceedings shall be considered preliminary, until such time as the allegations can be substantiated to the mutual satisfaction of everyone involved."

Well, perhaps not quite like Tirol, Wolff amended in thought. There, blame had been assigned—even though the guilty parties had escaped sentencing . . .

A month had passed since *The Homeward Bound* had folded from Earthspace, and the inquest had been going on for more than a week. Thus far, however, in trying to mount a case against the Shimadas, the GMP had only succeeded in muddying the waters. To establish beyond a reasonable doubt that Tokyo had manipulated the events would have required testimony from Kaaren Napperson. But dragging Napperson into court would have eventually led to the revelation that the GMP had given its tacit approval to the raid Vincinz's operatives had carried out against the Starchildren's colony.

As a means of safeguarding that same revelation, the intelligence agency had likewise been constrained to dismiss the charges of sedition leveled against Vincinz and the core membership of the Southern Cross command. Without evidence to corroborate that Vincinz had sinister designs on *The Homeward Bound*, the charges had been reduced to "unauthorized use of a Defense Force vessel," for which the general had received an official reprimand. Thanks to intense lobbying by Senator Grass—whose complicity in the hijacking could not be confirmed—the laser burst that had nearly atomized two Logans was ruled "inadvertent."

That left only Wolff, who had already been thoroughly interrogated by a brood of attorneys, and was next up, now that Kan Shimada's son had finished speaking. The stand was simply a podium positioned among tablefuls of lawyers, recording secretaries, and officers of the court. The inquest wasn't open to the public, though a few reporters had been granted permission to cover the proceedings for the media. Wolff often wondered how Catherine had reacted to seeing her estranged husband go from hero to accused.

Fredericks was handling the case for the GMP. Wolff's attorney, a small but ferocious young woman, had been appointed by the court.

"Colonel Wolff," Fredericks began when Wolff was in place, "to whom would you say you owe your allegiance as an officer in the Defense Force?"

Wolff frowned. "I'm not sure I understand the question."

Fredericks forced a thin smile. "What I mean is, you left Earth as a member of the Robotech Expeditionary Force, which answered to the Plenipotentiary Council, which itself was a judicial arm of the United Earth Government. But looking around this room, you'll find neither RDFers nor members of the Council. And our government, at this point, can scarcely be described as either united or global in scope. So, Colonel, to whom do you offer salute?"

Wolff touched his chin. "I suppose I'm still attached to the REF."

"And, in turn, to the Plenipotentiary Council, of which Dr. Emil Lang is a member in good standing."

"Lang and eleven others, yes."

"Very good, Colonel. And now that we've established that Lang is in effect your commander—one of twelve, at any rate—I want to return to something we discussed two days ago. You testified then that you had no knowledge of *The Homeward Bound*'s capacity for fold. And, I must say that your officers and crew have done an admirable job of bolstering your statements. However, I'd like to hear your explanation of why Dr. Lang and General Reinhardt opted to leave you uninformed as to the ship's fold potential."

Wolff addressed his response to the five judges seated opposite him. "I was simply charged with informing whomever was in command that the Masters' were en route to Earth. Unfortunately, I was too late. As to why Dr. Lang and General Reinhardt kept me in the dark," Wolff shrugged, "I guess they wanted me to remain on Earth at least until the computer time-released the fold codes."

"Then you have accepted Dana Sterling at her word regarding the hidden agenda of the ship's computer?"

"What reason would she have for lying?"

Fredericks snorted. "We'll come to that in a moment, Colonel. But before we do, could you elaborate on what you mean by the phrase 'whomever was in command.' "

Wolff took a breath. "Dr. Lang ventured that the Southern Cross apparat had ascended to a position of global authority, and that those in command would be reluctant to accept that General Edwards had joined forces with the enemy—the Invid Regent. He was further concerned that Edwards might pave the way for the invasion of Earth by the Invid Regent by making the most of his past affiliations."

Fredericks considered Wolff's words while he paced. "You're suggesting that General Edwards wouldn't be perceived as a threat by the people with whom he had been affiliated before the launch of the SDF-3."

"That's correct."

"Meaning who, Colonel? Which people, specifically?"

"Field Marshal Anatole Leonard, Chairman Wyatt Moran, and Dr. Lazlo Zand, among others."

Fredericks moved to the GMP table and picked up a sheet of paper. "This letter, handwritten and signed by Emil Lang, was provided to the court by Colonel Wolff, and it confirms his statements. But I would like him now to name the person to whom this letter was addressed."

"Rolf Emerson," Wolff said.

Fredericks repeated the name. "In other words, Colonel, you weren't ordered to deliver the information about the Masters, General Edwards, and the Invid to 'whomever was in command,' but to the highest-ranking member of the former Robotech Defense Force."

Wolff's lawyer shot to her feet. "Sirs, Colonel Fredericks is twisting the facts. Minister of Defense

Emerson was a major general in the Army of the Southern Cross."

Fredericks whirled on her. "Of late, perhaps. But until the Military Accord of 2030, Rolf Emerson was a career officer in the RDF."

As were Fredericks, Satori, and Aldershot, Wolff said to himself. But they were GMP now—Gimps, as they were sometimes called—movers and shakers in Earth's secret army, and seemed to have forgotten their roots.

"Colonel Fredericks, you're splitting hairs," one of the judges advised. "Southern Cross, Robotech Defense Force . . . Come to the point."

"The point, sirs, is that Colonel Wolff's primary responsibility was to keep his ship and the information it contained from *anyone* considered a rival of the Robotech Expeditionary Force. Isn't that true, Colonel?"

Wolff glared at Fredericks. "If it was, why would I have submitted to a full debriefing about the events on Tirol?"

Fredericks was willing to concede the point, but asked, "And you told the full truth during those debriefings?"

"Yes."

"And you likewise told us everything you knew about your ship?"

"Everything I knew."

Well, there it was, Wolff thought. He had just perjured himself. But as surely as he had encouraged Dana to take the ship, she had encouraged him to lie for the greater cause. *We all have our parts to play,* she had said to Aldershot before the fold, echoing Wolff's own words to her. And what a bittersweet event her departure had been for him, knowing he might never see her again.

The day she had come to his quarters, he had made a split-second decision to encourage her to take the ship. Once he had gotten over his initial anger and despondency, that was. But he had realized from her questions and tone of voice that the Shimada team had uncovered the truth about *The Homeward Bound*, and also that she had probably wired herself, in the hopes of conjuring the fold code out of him. So he had supplied it, though carefully, to avoid arousing the interests of the GMP personnel tasked with monitoring their conversation. Nor did he regard Dana's actions as a violation of trust, because she had attempted to tell him—in a code of her own devising—what she knew, and how conflicted she felt . . .

Fredericks was pacing once more, clearly building toward some bombshell. "Colonel Wolff, how would you characterize your relationship with Dana Sterling?" he asked suddenly. "Did you consider it a professional relationship?"

Wolff swallowed and said, "Yes." Because the GMP's surveillance tapes had been ruled admissible as evidence, he knew he had to exercise care.

"Strictly professional?"

"There was a personal side to it, as well. Relatively speaking, I was with her parents only a few months ago, and she was naturally curious to learn all she could about them."

"You told her that a second daughter had been born to Miriya Parino Sterling?"

"I did."

"And how did she take that news?"

"She was overjoyed."

"I imagine that she was anxious to meet her sibling."

"Why wouldn't she be?"

"Indeed, why wouldn't she be? . . . But getting back to the personal aspect of your relationship, how do you imagine that Dana Sterling saw you: as a fellow officer, a friend, a kind of father figure, a potential lover—"

"Colonel Fredericks," one of the judges interrupted. "This is an inquest, not a trial. Colonel Wolff is a decorated officer and I won't allow his name to be besmirched by innuendo."

Fredericks spent a few seconds studying his bloodless hands. "Sirs, if you'll permit me to proceed, the relevance of my questions will become apparent."

The judges conferred briefly. "We're going to allow you some leeway, Colonel," one of them said. "But I'm warning you, tread carefully."

Fredericks nodded. "Suppose we approach this from a different angle, Colonel Wolff. How would you characterize *your* feelings for Dana Sterling? She is, what— nineteen years old? And you're . . . Well, that's irrelevant, I'm sure. But just what did you feel toward her?"

"I thought of her as a valiant officer and a pleasant young woman."

"That's all—'a pleasant young woman?' I only ask because she made such a point of mentioning you in her final communication with General Aldershot. First, she absolves you of all complicity in the hijacking; then she suggests that we follow your advice concerning the Invid . . ."

"I can't help that," Wolff said brusquely.

"Then you don't feel she was going to great lengths to protect you?"

"Protect me from what?"

"Why, from *this*, Colonel. From a trial, in which you have been implicated as a conspirator. But, of course, you had no idea she was planning to hijack your ship."

Wolff grinned slightly. "I wasn't aware that it could be hijacked."

"I see ... So, during the moments the two of you spent together—aboard *The Homeward Bound* and ... elsewhere—Sterling merely plied you with questions about her parents and her baby sister. And perhaps she even told you that she missed them, terribly." Fredericks turned to Wolff. "Did she ever tell you that she missed them, Colonel?"

"She may have said that."

"And did she on any occasion tell you about the clones she was sheltering in Monument City."

"She spoke of them."

"Did you describe to you their desperate plight?"

"She said they were dying, if that's what you mean."

"And how did it affect you to hear about Sterling's longing to see her parents and the hopeless situation with the Tiroleans?"

"I felt bad for her."

Fredericks gazed at him. "Bad enough, Colonel, to supply the Shimadas with the fold codes for the ship, knowing full well that they would be passed on to Dana, who was herself desperate to reunite with her parents and save the lives of the Tiroleans she had taken under her wing?"

Wolff's lawyer jumped up. "Sirs, Colonel Wolff has already stated that he had no knowledge of the codes.

How many times are we going to cover the same ground?"

Fredericks made a placating gesture. "Colonel, didn't Sterling tell you that the Sensor Nebula couldn't be destroyed?"

"She did. But I didn't put any stock in what the Zentraedi said. For all I knew, they hated Dana for the role her mother played in the Malcontent Uprisings."

"Dana ..." Fredericks smiled nastily. "So you encouraged her to accept the Nebula mission—even though you and your crew had been excluded."

"I did. Strategically, it made sense to keep the Wolff Pack on Earth."

"Do you recall your words of encouragement to Sterling?"

"I think I said that she should do her best, and that she should take good care of the ship."

Fredericks approached Wolff and leaned on the podium, facing him. "Didn't you, in fact, tell her that she should use that ship as it was meant to be used?"

"I probably said something like that."

"Not 'probably,' Colonel. You said precisely that."

Fredericks turned an about-face. "And how was that ship meant to be used? As a two-way messenger. Colonel Wolff was sent to warn us about the Masters; that much is beyond dispute. But after discharging that responsibility, he was expected to return to Tirol. Separated from his ship, however, he had no choice but to send someone in his place. And that someone was Dana Sterling, with whom he had formed a ... paternalistic relationship.

"No sooner did he supply the fold codes to Tokyo, than Sterling began to concoct her scheme to loft the

Tiroleans to *The Homeward Bound*. She never had any intention of transferring them to the factory satellite, and I surmise that she only stopped there to take the surviving Zentraedi with her. Once aboard Wolff's ship, the Shimadas' machine assumed control. And the rest, sirs, is, as they say, history."

CHAPTER EIGHTEEN

> *It is also interesting to note that that year [2033] saw one of the mildest winters on record. This has been credited to the cloud of mecha and warship debris that had encircled Earth since the previous spring. But there are those who hold that the Flowers [of Life] themselves had an impact on the climate. They thrived because they had somehow convinced earth and sky to collaborate in their irruption.*
>
> Bloom Nesterfig, *Social Organization of the Invid*

T HE COURT DELIBERATED FOR A WEEK BEFORE RENdering its decision. Owing to a lack of evidence, Wolff was cleared of all charges. The Shimadas and Dana Sterling were found guilty of conspiracy and sedition, though the decision carried little weight, since there was nothing the court could do to either of them.

Confined to quarters, Wolff received the news on Denver Base, and immediately began packing his bags for a trip to Albuquerque. Catherine had invited him to visit her and Johnny, though Wolff hadn't been able to determine from the phone call whether she had had a change of heart or she simply felt sorry for him. Before he left Denver, however, Nova Satori requested that he meet with her—unofficially—to discuss matters of mutual concern. In her note, she had suggested a truck-stop restaurant on the Denver-Albuquerque highway, about twenty miles south of GMP headquarters, where she assured him they would both be safe from prying eyes and listening devices.

Wolff found her at the appointed time, in a tattered corner booth, ignoring the looks she was getting from a group of redneck drivers seated at the counter. The looks ceased when Wolff slipped into the booth, largely because Nova and Wolff seemed made for each other—an inseparable two of a kind.

"Thanks for coming," Nova said, leaning back in the booth to appraise him.

Wolff signaled for a waitress. When the waitress arrived, he ordered a coffee, then changed his mind. "Make that a beer—a tall one.

"What's on your mind, Satori?" He mirrored Nova's relaxed posture. "Want to tell me that you're not finished with me yet? That you won't rest until you see me in the brig?"

Nova scoffed at the idea. "Despite what you might think, Colonel, your freedom was never in jeopardy. Oh, we had to present that little mock inquest for the public's sake. But the outcome was never in question. You're a hero, and there aren't too many of you left. Especially now that Dana and her boys are on Tirol, or wherever your ship sent them."

Wolff inclined his head to one side. "Funny, I didn't feel much like a hero when Fredericks was grilling me."

Nova laughed shortly. "Come on, Colonel. We went easy on you." She narrowed her eyes. "We could have made a lot more of your 'paternalistic' relationship with Dana, for example."

"You should know, Satori. You were certainly watching me closely enough."

Nova shrugged. "Don't take it personally. It's simply part of what I do. Look at it this way: You probably wouldn't be off to see your wife right now if we'd revealed everything we knew."

Wolff shook his head in disgust. "You don't miss a trick. So, do we have matters of mutual concern to discuss, or did you get me here just to provoke me?"

"The former, Colonel. But first, answer one question: Would you have gone with the ship if you'd had the chance?"

"Back to Tirol?"

Nova nodded.

"No, I wouldn't have gone. I left my share of problems there. Anyway, somebody has to give you the straight dope on what we're up against with the Invid."

Nova smiled in grudging admiration. "You actually do give a damn about what happens here. You really are some kind of champion."

"Sorry to disappoint you."

"You haven't. In fact, you've made things a lot easier for me." She paused and leaned forward. "I want you to work for us, Wolff."

He gaped at her. "For the GMP? Are you nuts?"

"Maybe I am, but try to be objective for a minute and listen to what I have to say. The Defense Force is in shambles. Seventy-five percent of the Southern Cross units have decamped with their mecha and have formed scattered bands all across the North- and Southlands. But, as we're hearing it, many of those bands are in total agreement with you as to how to combat the Invid."

"That's encouraging," Wolff said tentatively.

"I agree. And it can be more than encouraging if you'd agree to act as our liaison in communicating with them. We have the makings of a resistance, but we have no one to organize it."

Wolff's beer arrived, and he took advantage of the moment to think things through. "Seems to me that those units decamped because they had no faith in the leadership of the Southern Cross," he said at last. "So what makes you think they'll listen to me if I'm suddenly a GMP officer?"

Nova shook her head. "You wouldn't be. You'll be a singleton. Plus, a figure to rally round. And all we'd expect from you in return is to be kept apprised of what you're doing—just so we can have some sense of our troop and mecha strengths."

"What do I get for my efforts? Aside from the expense account, I mean."

Nova folded her arms across her chest. "Now you're beginning to sound like the Jonathan Wolff I've read about. The one who made deals with Zentraedi malcontents just to get replacement parts for his Centaur tanks."

"Don't believe everything you read," Wolff advised.

"I'll remember that." Nova allowed a smile. "In any case, here's what we're prepared to offer you: funding for a base of operations for the Wolff Pack."

Wolff raised an eyebrow. "We'll require more than a base. We'll need mecha and Protoculture and the authority to expand our forces, however we see fit. I'd also want to include Major Carpenter in this."

"I can arrange that."

"And another thing: I want some assurance from Aldershot and the UEG that they're not going to go off half-cocked when the Regis shows up. If they do, we're lost—no matter what I manage to put together in the way of a resistance force."

"I'll talk to Aldershot," Nova said.

Wolff grinned, roguishly. "Then we just might be able to work together after all."

Nova returned the look. "When you . . . finish in Albuquerque, we'd like you to go to the Southlands. There's a group of ex-Southern Cross in Brasília who are calling themselves the Stonemen. We've had our problems with them in the past. But their commander, a guy named Gavin Murdock, intimated that he might be willing to talk terms, if you'd serve as a negotiator."

"Sounds like a reasonable first request," Wolff said.

"We'll furnish you with an Alpha. And while you're in the Southlands, give some thought to where you and the Wolff Pack might want to establish themselves. I suggest you check out a town called Valhalla, in central Amazonas. The Southern Cross had a base there before the War, in a crater left by a crashed Zentraedi warship."

"Valhalla," Wolff mused. "I think I already like it."

He lifted the beer to his lips and drained half the bottle.

"Kaaren's feeling is that the Invid will concentrate their hives in the Northlands, where the Flowers of Life are plentiful," Misa was telling Terry Weston as they stood in the wooden building that served as a terminal for the colony's airport. On the runway, the Shimada jet was being prepped for takeoff. Towering above the acacia and eucalyptus trees that bordered the asphalt strip was the dome that harbored *Napperson's Hope*. "Besides, there's no organized military presence in the Southlands. So the Invid might overlook us entirely."

"I hope you're right," Terry said, caressing Misa's right forearm. "But the Flowers have begun to blossom all around Buenos Aires, and that's not all that far from here."

"Kaaren's not saying that the Invid won't construct hives in the Southlands. But most of those will probably be far to the north, in the Venezuela Sector."

Terry snorted. "HEARTH country—which they're not going to surrender without a fight."

"So let them fight. So long as they leave us alone."

Terry had been in Argentina for over a month now, but with the inquest ended, it was time to return to Tokyo. From the start, the Shimadas had trusted that the GMP wouldn't subpoena testimony from Kaaren Napperson about the cult's ties to Tokyo—not if the GMP expected to conceal their hand in the raid that had damaged the saucer. But just to be on the safe side, Terry and several *yakuza* troubleshooters had been dispatched to the colony to make certain that Napperson didn't testify if summoned.

Misa had guessed the truth the moment Terry and the others had emerged from Kan Shimada's private jet, and she had spent the first two weeks vacillating between concern for Kaaren's safety and anger at the Family for once again resorting to intimidation. Terry supposed it was during that anxious period that she had made up her mind to remain with the colony and distance herself from the lush life she had known in the Tokyo geo-grid.

"I don't suppose I could get you to change your mind about staying here," Terry said, after a moment.

Misa shook her head. "I'm sick of Tokyo's ends-justifies-the-means mentality. We all want to survive, Terry. But the people here wouldn't sacrifice their ideals to ensure survival."

Terry grimaced. "They were ready to accept Wolff's ship when we offered it."

"Kaaren would never have allowed it, Terry. Okay, she didn't turn down Mr. Shimada's funds. But that was only to get the ship launched. Commandeering *The Homeward Bound* would have gone against everything the Starchildren stand for."

"And everything you stand for, it seems."

"I don't know how to feel about what everyone did to make sure *The Homeward Bound* would disappear. For all I know, Dana will return with the SDF-3 and the ends *will* have justified the means. But until then . . ." She sighed, then gazed at Terry. "Do you miss her?"

Terry hooked his long, blond hair behind his ears. "It's weird. I do miss her, but not in a private way. I think I miss not having her on Earth, if that makes any sense."

"Like she was a kind of lucky charm?"

"I'm not sure. But being with Dana always reminded me that we're not alone in the universe. That Human beings don't have any special claim to the stars."

Misa reigned in an amused smile. "You could always buy a telescope and stare at the factory satellite."

Terry laughed. "Maybe I will." He was quiet for a moment, then said, "What am I going to do when you leave?"

"Me? I'm not going anywhere. I didn't make the final cut."

"Is the new launch date set?"

"Three months from now."

"What are you going to do after it launches?"

She shrugged. "Help to build another one. Go on living the simple life. That's the real reason I'm not returning to Tokyo. I wasn't born to live in a tower. Fairy tales are all right to read, but not to live."

Terry took her hand once more. "You see? That's what I've always liked about you."

"Then you should stay here."

He rocked his head. "Who knows, I might come back. In the meantime, it sounds like you're well taken care of."

Misa had told him a little about Izumi Sasaki, but she blushed anyway. "I've finally found a home here—among people who aren't afraid of the future."

"Whatever gets you through the War," Terry said.

She nodded her head slowly, in thought. "When will they come?"

"Nobody seems to know—not even Wolff."

"At least we had the advantage of knowing that the Masters were on the way."

"This next one's going to be like the War against the Zentraedi: Lang and his Macross Island teams predicted that the owners of the SDF-1 would come looking for it, but they had no idea when that would happen. Substitute the Flowers of Life for the SDF-1 and we're back where we started."

"I keep thinking, if the Invid come, long-distance travel will probably be impossible." Misa bit her lower lip. "This could be the last time I see you, Terry."

He forced a laugh. "Tokyo will pull through. And so will this place. With the ship launched, how could the Invid regard you people as a threat?"

Misa's grin was slow in forming. "Even so, maybe I'll recommend to Kaaren that we should do as Mr. Shimada suggests: Welcome the Invid with bouquets of their Flowers."

"It doesn't look particularly sinister," Kan Shimada said of the triple-petaled flower Louie had handed him. They were standing under a tile-roofed pavilion of recent construction, which overlooked a broad valley, south of Tokyo, in the rain shadow of Mount Fuji.

Louie nodded uncertainly. "One person's beauty is another person's beast, sir."

"It is the nature of all things to possess a measure of good and a measure of evil," Kan replied. "But until I know differently, I shall elect to see only the good in this Flower, in the expectation that the Flower will repay me in kind."

Notwithstanding his remark, the head of the Shimada Family was wearing leather gloves that reached his elbows and a beekeeper's helmet. Louie had told him about the time Dana, Bowie, and Zor had ventured deep into the SDF-1 mound of the Macross trio and a Flower of Life had wrapped itself around Dana's arm like a predatory vine. Just the same, Louie was sorry he hadn't gone along on that jaunt; by the time he had gotten his first good look at the Flowers, they had already gone to seed.

Kan Shimada was turning the Flower about in his hand. "From this innocent-looking plant comes Protoculture," he mused.

Louie's eyes narrowed behind the tinted lenses of his goggles. "Comes war," he mumbled.

Once the hunting grounds of the Imperial family, the

rolling terrain was dotted with picturesque lakes, cypress groves, and the ruins of ancient temples and twentieth-century ski resorts. Many a Shimada Enterprises annual banquet had been held at a nearby inn, called the Gotenbu Onsen. But today the Family—sons, relatives, advisors, *otaku*, and researchers—were gathered to enact a ritual of a novel sort, one that was new to planet Earth, at any rate: a Flower of Life benediction.

A swath of fecund land in the valley had been cleared, leveled, and planted with triads of Flowers of Life seedlings, which in a few short weeks had grown to mature plants, pendulous with twisting buds that resembled elongated teardrops. And moving among them were a dozen Shinto priests, who, at Kan Shimada's request, had journeyed from Hakone Jinga, a sacred shrine on Fuji, that dated to the year A.D. 757. The priests were attired in saffron-colored robes, and they chanted as they wove among the clusters of Flowers. Some carried incense braziers or drums, and others wore finger cymbals.

Kan Shimada turned slightly to face Wilfred Gibley. "You are certain that the Flowers will thrive here?"

"Climatically, it's similar to the banana-belt valleys south of Macross and Monument City," Gibley answered. "Warm, sunny days; cool nights. Less rainfall, but the Flowers don't appear to be affected by underwatering. In fact, they seem to derive most of what they need from sunlight and from the ground—from the Earth itself."

Shimada lifted his face to the cirrus-streaked sky. "Winter is fast on the approach. We'll see how they fare when the weather changes."

A sudden, cool breeze ruffled Louie's hair. "Let's hope it's not too brutal a season."

Everyone fell silent for a long moment.

Below them, the buds and newly sprung petals of the Flowers bobbed and danced, as if in joyful anticipation of a long-overdue reunion ...

EPILOGUE

Astronomers who monitored the Sensor Nebula during the Invid occupation have reported that the "cloud" began to diminish in size and volume coincidental with the Regis's invasion, and continued to do so throughout that year [2033], until October, when it expanded to half its original size and underwent a series of changes in hue and reflectivity. Whether the changes were inspired by the arrival of the ships of the REF Mars Division has never been established. However, the Nebula did return to the Earth-proximal position it had reached during the final stages of the Masters' War [sic], only to be dispersed or destroyed the following year, along with the numerous ships that comprised the REF Tirol fleet.

General Marc J. Alan, as quoted in Maria Bartley-Rand, *Flower of Life: Journey Beyond Protoculture*

SINCE THE SURPRISE DEPARTURE OF *THE HOMEward Bound*, five months earlier, commo tech Paul Rawley, of Space Station Liberty had made a habit of speaking with the Zentraedi at least once during each of his shifts. Curious to know if Dana Sterling had executed a spacefold, Tay Wav'vir had initiated contact only hours after Wolff's ship had jumped; and from that first communication, a kind of radio friendship had formed between Rawley and the Micronized aliens. This had made it easier for him to accept the presence of the factory satellite in Earthspace, despite his continuing to regard it as a beacon for the Invid swarm.

The cloud, too—the so-called Sensor Nebula—was still lurking out by Mars orbit, looking from Earth like a postage stamp–size blemish of golden light. But the

enemy itself had yet to be heard from, and everyone
had begun to wonder if Dana Sterling's controversial
leave-taking hadn't resulted in some extraordinary oc-
currence in the far reaches of the Fourth Quadrant of
known space.

Not that the wondering had had any effect on Earth's
war footing. In fact, the Defense Force had succeeded
in reconditioning several *Tristar*-class battlewagons, and
rearming a dozen frigates and scores of Logans, Alphas,
Betas, Veritechs, Hovertanks, A-JACs, and other mecha.
Most of those, however, were being kept in concealment on the moon or on secret bases downside. And
even the fleet's spaceborne destroyers were separated
by great distances, so as not to present a visible threat
to the Invid.

Nevertheless, command's battle plan remained unclear. At times it appeared that a *limited* bombardment
of Earth would be tolerated before the fleet would be
directed to counterattack; but at other times—chiefly
when Southern Crossers were asked—one got the impression that any act of aggression would meet with an
immediate reply. The inconsistency troubled Rawley—
whose chronic anxiety was responding only sporadi-
cally to medication—and it was frequently the subject
of his conversations with Tay Wav'vir.

"You must cease your whining and honor your imperative," Tay was telling him during one seemingly in-
terminable shift in January 2033. The feed was audio
only, and Rawley often had to strain to hear her. "After
all, Paul Rawley, you are our eyes and ears on the Solar
System. We need you to alert us to the swarm's arrival,
so that we may fly to the fore."

The Zentraedi females had been armed, after a fashion, with six Battlepods that had been found moldering in a warehouse north of Detroit City.

"What can you hope to accomplish with six Battlepods?" Rawley asked.

"Distinction."

It was ground they had covered before, but no matter. Rawley was about to pursue the argument when the display screens at his station turned snow white. Tay picked up on his silence and asked the cause.

"Some kind of system glitch. The screens are white with interference."

"Pure white like the snow that falls in your northern climes?"

"Exactly like that. I'm going to—"

"Place your station on full alert," Tay interrupted. "The Regis has come. Empowered by the Flower of Life, she folds her brood through space-time by an effort of sheer will. Place your station on full alert, Rawley. The War has arrived."

Rawley's trembling hand opened a line to station control. "My screens are down," he started to say.

"We're working on it," the voice in his ear replied.

Rawley swallowed hard. "It's the Invid—they've *defolded*."

"Rawley, take it easy," the voice said after a moment. "A spacefold doesn't knock out every scanner on the station."

"I'm telling you, *it's the Invid*! Put the station on alert and notify ALUCE and Denver." His hand slammed down on the early warning keys. But no sirens answered him. "Put the station on alert!" he screamed.

The display screens had turned dazzling white and a circular, albescent glow was now visible through the observation bays, throwing the nearby factory satellite into stark silhouette.

Rawley's left hand fumbled for his vial of medication as a torchlike beam struck the factory satellite on its far side, instantly annihilating it. Then the beam sundered itself into more than a dozen curving combers that streaked downward to umbrella the Earth.

All but one, which was surging straight toward Liberty.

Within hours, Earth's major cities were lanced by the harnessed power of the Invid swarm. Contrary to what had been said, outlined, and sometimes promised, Defense Force command—in the moment it learned of the destruction of Space Station Liberty—ordered the fleet to counterattack. Teams of mecha launched from their places of concealment to engage the russet Pincer Units disgorged by the swarm's clam-shaped troop transports. The skies crackled with lightning and resounded with fulminations.

Incensed by the countless fiery deaths of her children, the Regis retaliated. Additional cities were targeted and reduced to rubble; then towns and villages; then anything that smacked of resistance: passenger jets and cargo ships, tractor trailers and heavy equipment, bullet trains and city buses ... She descended on the Starchildren's colony like a wrathful demon, killing thousands in one fell swoop and demolishing the ship that was to have launched the following week.

Earth was pounded and pulverized, rendered numb by the attack and the swiftness with which the swarm constructed their hives. Not only in the Northlands—whose tortured mid-Atlantic region was to house the Regis's sprawling, central-hive complex—but throughout the Southlands, and across the face of Europe and Asia, and southward into India, Indonesia, and Australia. Even Japan wasn't excluded. South of Tokyo, on the flanks of Mount Fuji, where they found fields of cultivated Flowers waiting for them, the Invid built several small stilt hives. Though they chose not to disturb the subterranean city nearby, treating it as if it were the nest of some innocuous indigenous species ...

Jonathan Wolff was in Brasília when the first enemy wave struck, but he made it safely back to Valhalla, or "Soldiertown," as the place had come to be called, where John Carpenter, the Wolff Pack, and hundreds of recruits were dug in, in anticipation of an attack that never came.

Months later, Carpenter would make a daring flight to Tokyo, returning to Valhalla with Louie Nichols, who helped reestablish contact with ALUCE, which had not been heard from since the first hours of the invasion. Plans were eventually devised for a coordinated attack on the central-hive complex—termed Reflex Point—to be led by General Nobutu's ALUCE forces, with support from Valhalla and the demoralized remnants of Aldershot and Satori's battalions.

But the attack would fail miserably, and would constitute the last action by Earth's ground forces for the remainder of 2032. Worse, the defeat would result in an irreparable breach in Wolff's forces, owing to Wolff's absence during the attack.

For days earlier, Wolff had learned that his wife and son were thought to be prisoners in a hive that had been constructed near the raging oil fires outside Dallas. Terry Weston—one of the few survivors of the

Starchildren's colony—would die in Wolff's raid on that hive. The assault, too, proved futile, in that Catherine and Johnny Wolff had already been moved to Reflex Point.

Carpenter would never forgive Wolff for putting his personal needs first. He would decamp for Portland and amass his own band of guerrilla fighters, known as the Splinters. Satori, too, would break ties with Wolff, withdrawing her support for Valhalla, which would slowly come to mirror the increasingly dissipated state of its disheartened commander.*

And as for Louie Nichols, he would remain in Valhalla for close to three months, returning to Tokyo soon after he had monitored a burst transmission from a Commander Gardner of the Mars Division. A fleet of REF ships had defolded from Tirol and were decelerating toward Earth.

In his brief communiqué, Gardner would not only make mention of admirals Rick Hunter and Lisa Hayes, General Gunther Reinhardt, and Dr. Emil Lang, but Dana Sterling and "the intrepid crew of *The Homeward Bound*."

The former 15th had succeeded.

And there was no stopping them now.

---

*Satori wouldn't surface again until after the war, as head of the so-called Homunculi Movement, although there would be evidence to suggest that the movement's leader was an imposter, and that the *real* Nova Satori was a secret though guiding force in Earth's Reconstruction.

You can't get
enough of the
exciting fantasy
and action in the
Robotech™
series books...

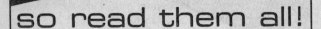

so read them all!

DEL REY ONLINE!

The Del Rey Internet Newsletter...

A monthly electronic publication, posted on the Internet, GEnie, CompuServe, BIX, various BBSs, and the Panix gopher (gopher.panix.com). It features hype-free descriptions of books that are new in the stores, a list of our upcoming books, special announcements, a signing/reading/convention-attendance schedule for Del Rey authors, "In Depth" essays in which professionals in the field (authors, artists, designers, sales people, etc.) talk about their jobs in science fiction, a question-and-answer section, behind-the-scenes looks at sf publishing, and more!

Online editorial presence: Many of the Del Rey editors are online, on the Internet, GEnie, CompuServe, America Online, and Delphi. There is a Del Rey topic on GEnie and a Del Rey folder on America Online.

Our official e-mail address for Del Rey Books is delrey@randomhouse.com

Internet information source!

A lot of Del Rey material is available to the Internet on a gopher server: all back issues and the current issue of the Del Rey Internet Newsletter, a description of the DRIN and summaries of all the issues' contents, sample chapters of upcoming or current books (readable or downloadable for free), submission requirements, mail-order information, and much more. We will be adding more items of all sorts (mostly new DRINs and sample chapters) regularly. The address of the gopher is gopher.panix.com

Why? We at Del Rey realize that the networks are the medium of the future. That's where you'll find us promoting our books, socializing with others in the sf field, and—most importantly—making contact and sharing information with sf readers.

For more information, e-mail delrey@randomhouse.com

WARNING!

VERY ADDICTIVE PRODUCTS!

PROTOCULTURE ADDICTS

THE ANIME & MANGA MAGAZINE

Discover Japanese animation & comics through synopses, reviews, interviews and articles on their place in Japanese culture. Get the latest news and learn what is really going on in the anime & manga world. The 56-page magazine now offers more coverage on mecha-oriented anime, their model kits, and all the other anime goods!

6 issues / year: $30

USA and OVERSEAS subscriptions must be in U.S. currency.
Canadians must add GST (7%) – For overseas subscriptions add $15.
Checks or money orders must be drawn to:

IANUS PUBLICATIONS, INC.
5000 Iberville, Suite 332, Montreal, Quebec, Canada, H2H 2S6.